I SAW THREE SHIPS

AND

OTHER WINTER'S TALES.

"IS IT BITTER, MY SON?"

"*I Saw Three Ships.*"—p. 102.

I SAW THREE SHIPS

AND

OTHER WINTER'S TALES.

BY

Sir Arthur Thomas Quiller-Couch

(Q, pseud.)

————•••————

Short Story Index Reprint Series

 BOOKS FOR LIBRARIES PRESS

FREEPORT, NEW YORK

First Published 1892
Reprinted 1971

118482

INTERNATIONAL STANDARD BOOK NUMBER:
0-8369-4023-7

LIBRARY OF CONGRESS CATALOG CARD NUMBER:
77-169560

PRINTED IN THE UNITED STATES OF AMERICA
BY
NEW WORLD BOOK MANUFACTURING CO., INC.
HALLANDALE, FLORIDA 33009

To

T. WEMYSS REID.

CONTENTS.

I SAW THREE SHIPS.

I SAW THREE SHIPS.

CHAPTER I.

THE FIRST SHIP.

In those west-country parishes where but a few years back the feast of Christmas Eve was usually prolonged with cake and cider, "crowding," and "geese dancing," till the ancient carols ushered in the day, a certain languor not seldom pervaded the services of the Church a few hours later. Red eyes and heavy, young limbs hardly rested from the *Dashing White Sergeant* and *Sir Roger*, throats husky from a plurality of causes — all these were recognised as proper to the season, and, in fact, of a piece with the holly on the communion rails.

On a dark and stormy Christmas morning as far back as the first decade of the century, this languor was neither more nor less apparent

than usual inside the small parish church of
Ruan Lanihale, although Christmas fell that
year on a Sunday, and dancing should, by
rights, have ceased at midnight. The building
stands high above a bleak peninsula on the
South Coast, and the congregation had struggled
up with heads slanted sou'-west against the
weather that drove up the Channel in a black
fog. Now, having gained shelter, they quickly
lost the glow of endeavour, and mixed in
pleasing stupor the humming of the storm in
the tower above, its intermittent onslaughts on
the leadwork of the southern windows, and the
voice of· Parson Babbage lifted now and again
from the chancel as if to correct the shambling
pace of the choir in the west gallery.

" Mark me," whispered Old Zeb Minards,
crowder and leader of the musicians, sitting back
at the end of the Psalms, and eyeing his fiddle
dubiously ; " If Sternhold be sober this morning, Hopkins be drunk as a fly, or 'tis t'other
way round."

" 'Twas middlin' wambly," assented Calvin
Oke, the second fiddle—a screw-faced man

tightly wound about the throat with a yellow kerchief.

"An' 'tis a delicate matter to cuss the singers when the musicianers be twice as bad."

"I'd a very present sense of being a bar or more behind the fair—that I can honestly vow," put in Elias Sweetland, bending across from the left. Now Elias was a bachelor, and had blown the serpent from his youth up. He was a bald, thin man, with a high leathern stock, and shoulders that sloped remarkably.

"Well, 'taint a suent engine at the best, Elias—that o' yourn," said his affable leader, "nor to be lightly trusted among the proper psa'ms, 'specially since Chris'mas three year, when we sat in the forefront of the gallery, an' you dropped all but the mouthpiece overboard on to Aunt Belovely's bonnet at 'I was glad when they said unto me.'"

"Aye, poor soul. It shook her. Never the same woman from that hour, I do b'lieve. Though I'd as lief you didn't mention it, friends, if I may say so; for 'twas a bitter portion."

Elias patted his instrument sadly, and the

three men looked up for a moment, as a scud
of rain splashed on the window, drowning a
sentence of the First Lesson.

" Well, well," resumed Old Zeb, " we all
have our random intervals, and a drop o' cider
in the mouthpieces is no less than Pa'son looks
for, Chris'mas mornin's."

" Trew, trew as proverbs."

" Howsever, 'twas cruel bad, that last psa'm,
I won't gainsay. As for that long-legged boy
o' mine, I keep silence, yea, even from hard
words, considerin' what's to come. But 'tis
given to flutes to make a noticeable sound,
whether tunable or false."

" Terrible shy he looks, poor chap ! "

The three men turned and contemplated
Young Zeb Minards, who sat on their left and
fidgeted, crossing and uncrossing his legs.

" How be feelin', my son ? "

" Very whitely, father ; very whitely, an'
yet very redly."

Elias Sweetland, moved by sympathy, handed
across a peppermint drop.

" Hee-hee ! " now broke in an octogenarian

treble, that seemed to come from high up in the head of Uncle Issy, the bass-viol player; " But cast your eyes, good friends, 'pon a little slip o' heart's delight down in the nave, and mark the flowers 'pon the bonnet nid-nodding like bees in a bell, with unspeakable thoughts."

" 'Tis the world's way wi' females."

" I'll wager, though, she wouldn't miss the importance of it—yea, not for much fine gold."

" Well said, Uncle," commented the crowder, a trifle more loudly as the wind rose to a howl outside : " Lord, how this round world do spin ! Simme 'twas last week I sat as may be in the corner yonder (I sang bass then), an' Pa'son Babbage by the desk statin' forth my own banns, an' me with my clean shirt collar limp as a flounder. As for your mother, Zeb, nuthin 'ud do but she must dream o' runnin' water that Saturday night, an' want to cry off at the church porch because 'twas unlucky. " Nothin' shall injuce me, Zeb," says she, and inside the half hour there she was glintin' fifty ways under her bonnet, to see how the rest o' the maidens was takin' it."

" Hey," murmured Elias, the bachelor; "but it must daunt a man to hear his name loudly coupled wi' a woman's before a congregation o' folks."

" 'Tis very intimate," assented Old Zeb.

But here the First Lesson ended. There was a scraping of feet, then a clearing of throats, and the musicians plunged into " *O, all ye works of the Lord.*"

Young Zeb, amid the moaning of the storm outside the building and the scraping and zooming of the instruments, string and reed, around him, felt his head spin ; but whether from the lozenge (that had suffered from the companionship of a twist of tobacco in Elias Sweetland's pocket), or the dancing last night, or the turbulence of his present emotions, he could not determine. Year in and year out, grey morning or white, a gloom rested always on the singers' gallery, cast by the tower upon the south side, that stood apart from the main building, connected only by the porch roof, as by an isthmus. And upon eyes used to this comparative obscurity the nave produced the effect of a bright parterre of flowers, especially in those days when all the women wore scarlet cloaks, to scare the French if they should invade. Zeb's gaze, amid the turmoil of sound, hovered around one such cloak, rested on a slim back resolutely turned to him, and a jealous bonnet, wandered to the bald scalp of Farmer Tresidder beside it, returned to Calvin Oke's sawing elbow and the long neck of Elias Sweetland bulging with the *fortissimo* of " O ye winds of God," then fluttered back to the red cloak.

These vagaries were arrested by three words from the mouth of Old Zeb, screwed sideways over his fiddle.

" Time—ye sawny ! "

Young Zeb started, puffed out his cheeks, and blew a shriller note. During the rest of the canticle his eyes were glued to the score, and seemed on the point of leaving their sockets with the vigour of the performance.

" Sooner thee'st married the better for us, my son," commented his father at the close ; " else farewell to psa'mody ! "

But Young Zeb did not reply. In fact, what

remained of the peppermint lozenge had somehow jolted into his windpipe, and kept him
occupied with the earlier symptoms of strangula-
tion.

His facial contortions, though of the liveliest,
were unaccompanied by sound, and, therefore,
unheeded. The crowder, with his eyes contem-
platively fastened on the capital of a distant
pillar, was pursuing a train of reflection upon
Church music; and the others regarded the
crowder.

"Now supposin', friends, as *I*'d a-fashioned
the wondrous words o' the ditty we've just
polished off; an' supposin' a friend o' mine,
same as Uncle Issy might be, had a-dropped in,
in passin', an' heard me read the same. ' Hullo ! '
he'd 'a said, ' You've a-put the same words
twice over.' ' How's that ? ' ' How's that ?
Why, here's *O ye Whales* (pointin' wi' his finger),
an' lo! again, *O ye Wells*.' ' 'T'aint the same,'
I'd ha' said. ' Well,' says Uncle Issy, ' 'tis *spoke*
so, anyways'——"

"Crowder, you puff me up," murmured
Uncle Issy, charmed with this imaginative and

wholly flattering sketch. "No—really now! Though, indeed, strange words have gone abroad before now, touching my wisdom : but I blow no trumpet."

"Such be your very words," the crowder insisted. "Now mark my answer. 'Uncle Issy,' says I, quick as thought, 'you dunder-headed old antic,—leave that to the musicianers. At the word 'whales,' let the music go snorty; an' for wells, gliddery; an' likewise in a moving dulcet manner for the holy an' humble Men o' heart.' Why, 'od rabbet us !—what's wrong wi' that boy?"

All turned to Young Zeb, from whose throat uncomfortable sounds were issuing. His eyes rolled piteously, and great tears ran down his cheeks.

"Slap en 'pon the back, Calvin : he's chuckin'."

"Ay—an' the pa'son at 'here endeth!'"

"Slap en, Calvin, quick ! For 'tis clunk or stuffle, an' no time to lose."

Down in the nave a light rustle of expect- ancy was already running from pew to pew as

B

Calvin Oke brought down his open palm with a
whack ! knocking the sufferer out of his seat,
and driving his nose smartly against the back-
rail in front.

Then the voice of Parson Babbage was lifted:
" I publish the Banns of marriage between
Zebedee Minards, bachelor, and Ruby Tresidder,
spinster, both of this parish. If any of you
know cause, or just impediment, why these two
persons——"

At this instant the church-door flew open,
as if driven in by the wind that tore up the
aisle in an icy current. All heads were turned.
Parson Babbage broke off his sentence and
looked also, keeping his forefinger on the flutter-
ing page. On the threshold stood an excited,
red-faced man, his long sandy beard blown
straight out like a pennon, and his arms moving
windmill fashion as he bawled—

" A wreck ! a wreck ! "

The men in the congregation leaped up.
The women uttered muffled cries, groped for
their husbands' hats, and stood up also. The
choir in the gallery craned forward, for the

church-door was right beneath them. Parson
Babbage held up his hand, and screamed out
over the hubbub—

"Where's she *to* ?"

"Under Bradden Point, an' comin' full tilt
for the Raney ! "

"Then God forgive all poor sinners aboard ! "
spoke up a woman's voice, in the moment's
silence that followed.

"Is that all you know, Gauger Hocken ? "

"Iss, iss: can't stop no longer—must be off
to warn the Methodeys! 'Stablished Church
first, but fair play's a jewel, say I."

He rushed off inland towards High Lanes,
where the meeting-house stood. Parson Babbage
closed the book without finishing his sentence,
and his audience scrambled out over the graves
and forth upon the headland. The wind here
came howling across the short grass, blowing
the women's skirts wide and straining their
bonnet-strings, pressing the men's trousers tight
against their shins as they bent against it in
the attitude of butting rams and scanned the
coast-line to the sou'-west. Ruby Tresidder, on

gaining the porch, saw Young Zeb tumble out
of the stairway leading from the gallery and run
by, stowing the pieces of his flute in his pocket
as he went, without a glance at her. Like all
the rest, he had clean forgotten the banns.

Now, Ruby was but nineteen, and had
seen plenty of wrecks, whereas these banns were
to her an event of singular interest, for weeks
anticipated with small thrills. Therefore, as the
people passed her by, she felt suddenly out of
tune with them, especially with Zeb, who, at
least, might have understood her better. Some
angry tears gathered in her eyes at the callous
indifference of her father, who just now was
revolving in the porch like a weathercock, and
shouting orders east, west, north, and south for
axes, hammers, ladders, cart-ropes, in case the
vessel struck within reach

"You, Jim Lewarne, run to the mowhay,
hot-foot, an' lend a hand wi' the datchin' ladder,
an'—hi! stop!—fetch along my second-best
glass, under the Dook o' Cumberland's picter i'
the parlour, 'longside o' last year's neck; an'—
hi! cuss the chap—he's gone like a Torpointer!

Ruby, my dear, step along an' show en—Why, hello !——"

Ruby, with head down, and scarlet cloak blown out horizontally, was already fighting her way out along the headland to a point where Zeb stood, a little apart from the rest, with both palms shielding his eyes.

" Zeb ! "

She had to stand on tip-toe and bawl this into his ear. He faced round with a start, nodded as if pleased, and bent his gaze on the Channel again.

Ruby looked too. Just below, under veils of driving spray, the seas were thundering past the headland into Ruan Cove. She could not see them break, only their backs swelling and sinking, and the puffs of foam that shot up like white smoke at her feet and drenched her gown. Beyond, the sea, the sky, and the irregular coast with its fringe of surf melted into one uniform grey, with just the summit of Bradden Point, two miles away, standing out above the wrack. Of the vessel there was, as yet, no sign.

In Ruby's present mood the bitter blast was

chiefly blameworthy for gnawing at her face, and the spray for spoiling her bonnet and taking her hair out of curl. She stamped her foot and screamed again—

" Zeb ! "

" What is't, my dear ? " he bawled back in her ear, kissing her wet cheek in a preoccupied manner.

She was about to ask him what this wreck amounted to, that she should for the moment sink to nothing in comparison with it. But, at this instant, a small group of men and women joined them, and, catching sight of the faces of Sarah Ann Nanjulian and Modesty Prowse, her friends, she tried another tack—

" Well, Zeb, no doubt 'twas disappointing for you ; but don't 'ee take on so. Think how much harder 'tis for the poor souls i' that ship."

This astute sentence, however, missed fire completely. Zeb answered it with a point-blank stare of bewilderment. The others took no notice of it whatever.

" Hav'ee seen her, Zeb ? " called out his father.

" No."

" Nor I nuther. 'Reckon 'tis all over a'ready. I've a-heard afore now," he went on, turning his back to the wind the better to wink at the company, " that 'tis lucky for some folks Gauger Hocken bain't extra spry 'pon his pins. But 'tis a gift that cuts both ways. Be any gone round by Cove Head to look out ? "

" Iss, a dozen or more. I saw 'em 'pon the road, a minute back, like emmets runnin'. "

" 'Twas very nice feelin', I must own—very nice indeed—of Gauger Hocken to warn the church-folk first; and him a man of no faith, as you may say. Hey? What's that? Dost see her, Zeb ? "

For Zeb, with his right hand pressing down his cap, now suddenly flung his left out in the direction of Bradden Point. Men and women craned forward.

Below the distant promontory, a darker speck had started out of the medley of grey tones. In a moment it had doubled its size—had become a blur—then a shape. And at length, out of the leaden wrack, there emerged a small schooner, with tall, raking masts, flying straight towards them.

"Dear God!" muttered some one, while Ruby dug her finger-tips into Zeb's arm.

The schooner raced under bare poles, though a strip or two of canvas streamed out from her fore-yards. Yet she came with a rush like a greyhound's, heeling over the whitened water, close under the cliffs, and closer with every instant. A man, standing on any one of the points she cleared so narrowly, might have tossed a pebble on to her deck.

"Hey, friends, but she'll not weather Gaffer's Rock. By crum! if she does, they may drive her in 'pon the beach, yet!"

"What's the use, i' this sea? Besides, her steerin' gear's broke," answered Zeb, without moving his eyes.

This Gaffer's Rock was the extreme point of the opposite arm of the cove—a sharp tooth rising ten feet or more above high-water mark. As the little schooner came tearing abreast of it, a huge sea caught her broadside, and lifted as if to fling her high and dry. The men and women on the headland held their breath while she hung on its apex. Then she toppled and plunged across the mouth of the cove, quivering. She must have shaved the point by a foot.

" The Raney! the Raney!" shouted young Zeb, shaking off Ruby's clutch. "The Raney, or else——"

He did not finish his sentence, for the stress of the flying seconds choked down his words. Two possibilities they held, and each big with doom. Either the schooner must dash upon the Raney—a reef, barely covered at high water, barring entrance to the cove—or avoiding this, must be shattered on the black wall of rock under their very feet. The end of the little vessel was written—all but one word: and that must be added within a short half-minute.

Ruby saw this: it was plain for a child to read. She saw the curded tide, now at half-flood, boiling around the Raney; she saw the little craft swoop down on it, half buried in the seas through which she was being impelled; she saw distinctly one form, and one only, on the deck beside the helm—a form that flung up its hands as it shot by the smooth edge of the reef, a hand's-breadth off destruction. The hands were still lifted as it passed under the ledge where she stood.

It seemed, as she stood there shivering, covering her eyes, an age before the crash came, and the cry of those human souls in their extremity.

When at length she took her hands from her face the others were twenty yards away, and running fast.

CHAPTER II.

THE SECOND SHIP.

FATE, which had freakishly hurled a ship's crew
out of the void upon this particular bit of coast,
as freakishly preserved them.

The very excess of its fury worked this
wonder. For the craft came in on a tall billow
that flung her, as a sling might, clean against
the cliff's face, crumpling the bowsprit like
paper, sending the foremast over with a crash,
and driving a jagged tooth of rock five feet into
her ribs beside the breastbone. So, for a
moment it left her, securely gripped and bump-
ing her sternpost on the ledge beneath. As the
next sea deluged her, and the next, the folk
above saw her crew fight their way forward up
the slippery deck, under sheets of foam. With
the fifth or six wave her mizen-mast went; she
split open amidships, pouring out her cargo.
The stern slipped off the ledge and plunged

twenty fathoms down out of sight.   And now
the fore-part alone remained—a piece of deck,
the stump of the foremast, and five men clinging in a tangle of cordage, struggling up and
toppling back as each successive sea soused over
them.

Three men had detached themselves from
the group above the cliff, and were sidling down
its face cautiously, for the hurricane now flat-
tened them back against the rock, now tried to
wrench them from it; and all the way it was a
tough battle for breath.   The foremost was Jim
Lewarne, Farmer Tresidder's hind, with a coil
of the farmer's rope slung round him.   Young
Zeb followed, and Elias Sweetland, both simi-
larly laden.

Less than half-way down the rock plunged
abruptly, cutting off farther descent.

Jim Lewarne, in a cloud of foam, stood up,
slipped the coil over his head, and unwound it,
glancing to right and left.   Now Jim amid
ordinary events was an acknowledged fool, and
had a wife to remind him of it; but perch him
out of female criticism, on a dizzy foothold such

as this, and set him a desperate job, and you clarified his wits at once. This eccentricity was so notorious that the two men above halted in silence, and waited.

Jim glanced to right and left, spied a small pinnacle of rock about three yards away, fit for his purpose, sidled towards it, and, grasping, made sure that it was firm. Next, reeving one end of the rope into a running noose, he flung it over the pinnacle, and with a tug had it taut. This done, he tilted his body out, his toes on the ledge, his weight on the rope, and his body inclined forward over the sea at an angle of some twenty degrees from the cliff.

Having by this device found the position of the wreck, and judging that his single rope would reach, he swung back, gained hold of the cliff with his left hand, and with his right caught and flung the leaded end far out. It fell true as a bullet, across the wreck. As it dropped, a sea almost swept it clear; but the lead hitched in a tangle of cordage by the port cathead; within twenty seconds the rope was caught and made fast below.

All was now easy.   At a nod from Jim
young Zeb passed down a second line, which
was lowered along the first by a noose.   One by
one the whole crew—four men and a cabin-boy
—were hauled up out of death, borne off to the
vicarage, and so pass out of our story.

Their fate does not concern us, for this
reason—men with a narrow horizon and no
wings must accept all apparent disproportions
between cause and effect.   A railway collision
has other results besides wrecking an ant-hill,
but the wise ants do not pursue these in the
Insurance Reports.   So it only concerns us that
the destruction of the schooner led in time to
a lovers' difference between Ruby and young
Zeb—two young people of no eminence outside
of these pages.   And, as a matter of fact, her
crew had less to do with this than her cargo.

She had been expressly built by Messrs.
Taggs & Co., a London firm, in reality as a
privateer (which explains her raking masts), but
ostensibly for the Portugal trade ; and was
homeward bound from Lisbon to the Thames,
with a cargo of red wine and chestnuts.   At

Falmouth, where she had run in for a couple of days, on account of a damaged rudder, the captain paid off his extra hands, foreseeing no difficulty in the voyage up Channel. She had not, however, left Falmouth harbour three hours before she met with a gale that started her steering-gear afresh. To put back in the teeth of such weather was hopeless; and the attempt to run before it ended as we know.

When Ruby looked up, after the crash, and saw her friends running along the headland to catch a glimpse of the wreck, her anger returned. She stood for twenty minutes at least, watching them; then, pulling her cloak closely round her, walked homewards at a snail's pace. By the church gate she met the belated Methodists hurrying up, and passed a word or two of information that sent them panting on. A little beyond, at the point where the peninsula joins the mainland, she faced round to the wind again for a last glance. Three men were following her slowly down the ridge with a burden between them. It was the first of the rescued crew—a lifeless figure wrapped in oil-skins, with one arm hanging limply down, as if broken. Ruby halted, and gave time to come up.

"Hey, lads," shouted Old Zeb, who walked first, with a hand round each of the figure's sea-boots; "now that's what I'd call a proper womanly masterpiece, to run home to Sheba an' change her stockings in time for the randi-voose."

"I don't understand," said his prospective daughter-in-law, haughtily.

"O boundless depth! Rest the poor mortal down, mates, while I take breath to humour her. Why, my dear, you must know from my tellin' that there *hev* a-been such a misfortunate goin's on as a wreck, hereabouts."

He paused to shake the rain out of his hat and whiskers. Ruby stole a look at the oil-skin. The sailor's upturned face was of a sickly yellow, smeared with blood and crusted with salt. The same white crust filled the hollows of his closed eyes, and streaked his beard and hair. It turned her faint for the moment.

"An' the wreck's scat abroad," continued Old Zeb; an' the interpretation thereof is barrels an' nuts. What's more, tide'll be runnin' for two hour yet; an' it hasn' reached my ears that the fashion of thankin' the Lord for His bounty have a-perished out o' this old-fangled race of men an' women; though no doubt, my dear, you'd get first news o' the change, with a bed-room window facin' on Ruan Cove."

"Thank you, Old Zeb; I'll be careful to draw my curtains," said she, answering sarcasm with scorn, and turning on her heel.

The old man stooped to lift the sailor again. "Better clog your pretty ears wi' wax," he called after her, "when the kiss-i'-the-ring begins! Well-a-fine! What a teasin' armful is woman, afore the first-born comes! Hey, Sim Udy? Speak up, you that have fifteen to feed."

"Ay, I was a low feller, first along," answered Sim Udy, grinning. "'Sich common notions, Sim, as you do entertain!' was my wife's word."

"Well, souls, we was a bit tiddlywinky last

c

Michaelmas, when the *Young Susannah* came
ashore, that I must own. Folks blamed the
Pa'son for preachin' agen it the Sunday after.
'A disreppitable scene,' says he, ''specially
seein' you had nowt to be thankful for but a
cargo o' sugar that the sea melted afore you
could get it.' (Lift the pore chap aisy, Sim.)
By crum! Sim, I mind your huggin' a staved
rum cask, and kissin' it, an' cryin', 'Aw, Ben—
dear Ben!' an' 'After all these years!' fancyin'
'twas your twin brother come back, that was
killed aboard the *Agamemny*——"

"Well, well—prettily overtook I must ha'
been. (Stiddy, there, Crowder, wi' the legs of
en.) But to-day I'll be mild, as 'tis Chris'mas."

"Iss, iss; be very mild, my sons, as 'tis so
holy a day."

They tramped on, bending their heads at
queer angles against the weather, that erased
their outlines in a bluish mist, through which
they loomed for a while at intervals, until they
passed out of sight.

Ruby, meanwhile, had hurrie1 on, her cloak
flapping loudly as it grew heavier with moisture,

and the water in her shoes squishing at every step. At first she took the road leading down-hill to Ruan Cove, but turned to the right after a few yards, and ran up the muddy lane that was the one approach to Sheba, her father's farm.

The house, a square, two-storeyed building of greystone, roofed with heavy slates, was guarded in front by a small courtlage, the wall of which blocked all view from the lower rooms. From the narrow mullioned windows on the upper floor, however, one could look over it upon the duck-pond across the road, and down across two grass meadows to the cove. A white gate opened on the courtlage, and the path from this to the front door was marked out by slabs of blue slate, accurately laid in line. Ruby, in her present bedraggled state, avoided the front entrance, and followed the wall round the house to the town-place, stopping on her way to look in at the kitchen window.

" Mary Jane, if you call that a roast goose, I call it a burning shame ! "

Mary Jane, peeling potatoes with her back

c 2

to the window, and tossing them one by one into a bucket of water, gave a jump, and cut her finger, dropping forthwith a half-peeled magnum bonum, which struck the bucket's edge and slid away across the slate flooring under the table.

"Awgh—awgh!" she burst out, catching up her apron and clutching it round the cut. "Look what you've done, Miss Ruby! an' me miles away, thinkin' o' shipwrecks an' dead swollen men."

"Look at the Chris'mas dinner, you mazed creature!"

In truth, the goose was fast spoiling. The roasting apparatus in this kitchen was a simple matter, consisting of a nail driven into the centre of the chimney-piece, a number of worsted threads depending therefrom, and a steel hook attached to these threads. Fix the joint or fowl firmly on the hook, give it a spin with the hand, and the worsted threads wound, unwound, and wound again, turning it before the blaze—an admirable jack, if only looked after. At present it hung motionless over the dripping-pan, and the goose wore a suit of motley, exhibiting a rich Vandyke brown to the fire, an unhealthy yellow to the window.

"There now!" Mary Jane rushed to the jack and gave it a spin, while Ruby walked round by the back door, and appeared dripping on the threshold. "I declare 'tis like Troy Town this morning : wrecks and rumours o' wrecks Now 'tis ' Ropes! ropes!' an' nex' 'tis 'Where be the stable key, Mary Jane, my dear?' an' then agen, ' Will'ee be so good as to fetch master's second-best spy-glass, Mary Jane, an' look slippy?'—an' me wi' a goose to stuff, singe, an' roast, an' 'tatties to peel, an' greens to cleanse, an' apples to chop for sauce, an' the hoarders no nearer away than the granary loft, with a gatherin' 'pon your second toe an' the half o' 'em rotten when you get there. The pore I be in! Why, Miss Ruby, you'm streamin'-leakin'!"

"I'm wet through, Mary Jane ; an' I don't care if I die." Ruby sank on the settle, and fairly broke down.

"Hush 'ee now, co!"

"I don't, I don't, an' I don't! I'm tired o'

the world, an' my heart's broke. Mary Jane, you selfish thing, you've never asked about my banns, no more'n the rest; an' after that cast-off frock, too, that I gave you last week so good as new!"

"Was it very grand, Miss Ruby? Was it shuddery an' yet joyful—lily-white an' yet rosy-red—hot an' yet cold—'don't lift me so high,' an' yet 'praise God, I'm exalted above women'?"

"'Twas all and yet none. 'Twas a voice speakin' my name, sweet an' terrible, an' I longed for it to go on an' on; and then came the Gauger stunnin' and shoutin' 'Wreck! wreck!' like a trumpet; an' the church was full o' wind, an' the folk ran this way an' that, like sheep, an' left me sittin' there. I'll—I'll die an old maid, I will, if only to s—spite such ma—ma—manners!"

"Aw, pore dear! But there's better tricks than dyin' unwed. Bind up my finger, Miss Ruby, an' listen. You shall play Don't Care, an' change your frock, an' we'll step down to th' cove after dinner an' there be heartless and fancy-free. Lord! when the dance strikes up, to see you carryin' off the other maids' danglers an' treating your own man like dirt!"

Ruby stood up, the water still running off her frock upon the slates, her moist eyes resting beyond the window on the midden-heap across the yard, as if she saw there the picture Mary Jane conjured up.

"No. I won't join their low frolic; an' you ought to be above it. I'll pull my curtains an' sit up-stairs all day, an' you shall read to me."

The other pulled a wry face. This was not her idea of enjoyment. She went back to the goose sad at heart, for Miss Ruby had a knack of enforcing her wishes.

Sure enough, soon after dinner was cleared away (a meal through which Ruby had sulked and Farmer Tresidder eaten heartily, talking with a full mouth about the rescue, and coarsely ignoring what he called his daughter's "faddles"), the two girls retired to the chamber up-stairs; where the mistress was as good as her word, and pulled the dimity curtains before settling herself down in an easy-chair to listen to extracts from a polite novel as rendered aloud, under dire compulsion, by Mary Jane.

The rain had ceased by this, and the wind abated, though it still howled around the angle of the house and whipped a spray of the monthly-rose bush on the quarrels of the window, filling the pauses during which Mary Jane wrestled with a hard word. Ruby herself had taught the girl this accomplishment—rare enough at the time—and Mary Jane handled it gingerly, beginning each sentence in a whisper, as if awed by her own intrepidity, and ending each in a kind of gratulatory cheer. The work was of that class of epistolary fiction then in vogue, and the extract singularly well fitted to Ruby's mood.

"My dearest Wil-hel-mina," began Mary Jane, "racked with a hun-dred conflicting em-otions, I resume the nar-rative of those fa-tal moments which rapt me from your affec-tion-ate em-brace. Suffer me to re—to re-cap——"

"Better spell it, Mary Jane."

"To r.e., re— c.a.p., cap, recap— i.t, it, re-

capit— Lor'! what a twister!—u, recapitu—l.a.t.e,
late, re-cap-it-u-late the events de-tailed in my
last letter, full stop—there! if I han't read that
full stop out loud! Lord Bel-field, though an
ad-ept in all the arts of dis-sim-u-la-tion (and
how of-ten do we not see these arts al-lied with
un-scru-pu-lous pas-sions?), was un-able to
sus-tain the gaze of my in-fu-ri-a-ted pa-pa,
though he com-port-ed himself with suf-fic-ient
p.h.l.e.g.m—Lor'! what a funny word!"

Ruby yawned. It is true she had drawn the
dimity curtains—all but a couple of inches.
Through this space she could see the folk busy
on the beach below like a swarm of small black
insects, and continually augmented by those
who, having run off to snatch their Christmas
dinner, were returning to the spoil. Some
lined the edge of the breakers, waiting the
moment to rush in for a cask or spar that the
tide brought within reach; others (among
whom she seemed to descry Young Zeb) were
clambering out with grapnels along the western
rocks; a third large group was gathered in the
very centre of the beach, and from the midst of

these a blue wreath of smoke began to curl up. At the same instant she heard the gate click outside, and pulling the curtain wider, saw her father trudging away down the lane.

Mary Jane, glancing up, and seeing her mistress crane forward with curiosity, stole behind and peeped over her shoulder.

" I declare they'm teening a fire ! "

" Who gave you leave to bawl in my ear so rudely ? Go back to your reading, this instant." (A pause.) " Mary Jane, I do believe they'm roastin' chestnuts."

" What a clever game ! "

" Father said at dinner the tide was bringin' 'em in by bushels. Quick ! put on your worst bonnet an' clogs, an' run down to look. I *must* know. No, I'm not goin'—the idea ! I wonder at your low notions. You shall bring me word o' what's doin'—an' mind you're back before dark."

Mary Jane fled precipitately, lest the order should be revoked. Five minutes later, Ruby heard the small gate click again, and with a sigh saw the girl's rotund figure waddling down the

lane. Then she picked up the book and strove
to bury herself in the woes of Wilhelmina, but
still with frequent glances out of window.
Twice the book dropped off her lap; twice she
picked it up and laboriously found the page
again. Then she gave it up, and descended to
the back door, to see if anyone were about who
might give her news. But the town-place was
deserted by all save the ducks, the old white sow,
and a melancholy crew of cocks and hens huddled
under the dripping eaves of the cow-house.
Returning to her room, she settled down on the
window-seat, and watched the blaze of the
. bonfire increase as the short day faded.

The grey became black. It was six o'clock,
and neither her father nor Mary Jane had
returned. Seven o'clock struck from the tall
clock in the kitchen, and was echoed ten minutes
after by the Dutch clock in the parlour below.
The sound whirred up through the planching
twice as loud as usual. It was shameful to be
left alone like this, to be robbed, murdered, goodness knew what. The bonfire began to die out,
but every now and then a circle of small black

figures would join hands and dance round it, scattering wildly after a moment or two. In a lull of the wind she caught the faint sound of shouts and singing, and this determined her.

She turned back from the window and groped for her tinder-box. The glow, as she blew the spark upon the dry rag, lit up a very pretty but tear-stained pair of cheeks ; and when she touched off the brimstone match, and, looking up, saw her face confronting her, blue and tragical, from the dark-framed mirror, it reminded her of Lady Macbeth. Hastily lighting the candle, she caught up a shawl and crept down-stairs. Her clogs were in the hall ; and four horn lanterns dangled from a row of pegs above them. She caught down one, lit it, and throwing the shawl over her head, stepped out into the night.

The wind was dying down and seemed almost warm upon her face. A young moon fought gallantly, giving the massed clouds just enough light to sail by ; but in the lane it was dark as pitch. This did not so much matter, as the rain had poured down it like a sluice, washing the flints clean. Ruby's lantern swung to and fro, casting a yellow glare on the tall hedges, drawing queer gleams from the holly-bushes, and flinging an ugly, amorphous shadow behind, that dogged her like an enemy.

At the foot of the lane she could clearly distinguish the songs, shouts, and shrill laughter, above the hollow roar of the breakers.

"They're playin' kiss-i'-the-ring. That's Modesty Prowse's laugh. I wonder how any man *can* kiss a mouth like Modesty Prowse's!"

She turned down the sands towards the bonfire, grasping as she went all the details of the scene.

In the glow of the dying fire sat a semicircle of men—Jim Lewarne, sunk in a drunken slumber, Calvin Oke bawling in his ear, Old Zeb on hands and knees, scraping the embers together, Toby Lewarne (Jim's elder brother) thumping a pannikin on his knee and bellowing a carol, and a dozen others—in stages varying from qualified sobriety to stark and shameless intoxication—peering across the fire at the game in progress between them and the faint line that marked where sand ended and sea began.

"Zeb's turn!" roared out Toby Lewarne, breaking off *The Third Good Joy* midway, in his excitement.

"Have a care—have a care, my son!" Old Zeb looked up to shout. "Thee'rt so good as wed already; so do thy wedded man's duty, an' kiss th' hugliest!"

It was true. Ruby, halting with her lantern a pace or two behind the dark semicircle of backs, saw her perfidious Zeb moving from right to left slowly round the circle of men and maids that, with joined hands and screams of laughter, danced as slowly in the other direction. She saw him pause once—twice, feign to throw the kerchief over one, then still pass on, calling out over the racket :—

> "*I sent a letter to my love,*
> *I carried water in my glove,*
> *An' on the way I dropped it—dropped it—*
> *dropped it—*"

He dropped the kerchief over Modesty Prowse.

"ZEB!"

Young Zeb whipped the kerchief off Modesty's neck, and spun round as if shot.

The dancers looked; the few sober men by the fire turned and looked also.

" 'Tis Ruby Tresidder!" cried one of the girls; "'Wudn' be i' thy shoon, Young Zeb, for summat."

Zeb shook his wits together and dashed off towards the spot, twenty yards away, where Ruby stood holding the lantern high, its ray full on her face. As she started she kicked off her clogs, turned, and ran for her life.

Then, in an instant, a new game began upon the sands. Young Zeb, waving his kerchief and pursuing the flying lantern, was turned, baffled, intercepted—here, there, and everywhere —by the dancers, who scattered over the beach with shouts and peals of laughter, slipping in between him and his quarry. The elders by the fire held their sides and cheered the sport. Twice Zeb was tripped up by a mischievous boot, floundered and went sprawling; and the roar was loud and long. Twice he picked himself up and started again after the lantern, that

zig-zagged now along the fringe of the waves,
now up towards the bonfire, now off along the
dark shadow of the cliffs.

Ruby could hardly sift her emotions when
she found herself panting and doubling in
flight. The chase had started without her
will or dissent; had suddenly sprung, as it
were, out of the ground. She only knew that
she was very angry with Zeb; that she longed
desperately to elude him; and that he must
catch her soon, for her breath and strength were
ebbing.

What happened in the end she kept in her
dreams till she died. Somehow she had dropped
the lantern and was running up from the sea
towards the fire, with Zeb's feet pounding
behind her, and her soul possessed with the
dread to feel his grasp upon her shoulders. As
it fell, Old Zeb leapt up to his feet with excitement, and opened his mouth wide to cheer.

But no voice came for three seconds: and
when he spoke this was what he said—

" Good Lord, deliver us ! "

She saw his gaze pass over her shoulder;

and then heard these words come slowly, one by one, like dropping stones. His face was like a ghost's in the bonfire's light, and he muttered again—" From battle and murder, and from sudden death—Good Lord, deliver us ! "

She could not understand at first; thought it must have something to do with Young Zeb, whose arms were binding hers, and whose breath was hot on her neck. She felt his grasp relax, and faced about.

Full in front, standing out as the faint moon showed them, motionless, as if suspended against the black sky, rose the masts, yards, and square-sails of a full-rigged ship.

The men and women must have stood a whole minute—dumb as stones—before there came that long curdling shriek for which they waited. The great masts quivered for a second against the darkness; then heaved, lurched, and reeled down, crashing on the Raney.

D

CHAPTER III.

THE STRANGER.

As the ship struck, night closed down again, and her agony, sharp or lingering, was blotted out. There was no help possible ; no arm that could throw across the three hundred yards that separated her from the cliffs ; no swimmer that could carry a rope across those breakers ; nor any boat that could, with a chance of life, put out among them. Now and then a dull crash divided the dark hours, but no human cry again reached the shore.

Day broke on a grey sea still running angrily, a tired and shivering group upon the beach, and on the near side of the Raney a shapeless fragment, pounded and washed to and fro—a relic on which the watchers could in their minds re-build the tragedy.

The Raney presents a sheer edge to sea-ward—an edge under which the first vessel, though almost grazing her side, had driven in plenty of water. Shorewards, however, it descends by gradual ledges. Beguiled by the bonfire, or mistaking Ruby's lantern for the tossing stern-light of a comrade, the second ship had charged full-tilt on the reef and hung herself upon it, as a hunter across a fence. Before she could swing round, her back was broken; her stern parted, slipped back and settled in many fathoms; while the fore-part heaved forwards, toppled down the reef till it stuck, and there was slowly brayed into pieces by the seas. The tide had swept up and ebbed without dislodging it, and now was almost at low-water mark.

"'May so well go home to breakfast," said Elias Sweetland, grimly, as he took in what the uncertain light could show.

"Here, Young Zeb, look through my glass," sang out Farmer Tresidder, handing the telescope. He had been up at the vicarage drinking hot grog with the parson and the rescued men, when Sim Udy ran up with news of the fresh disaster; and his first business on descending to

D 2

118482

the Cove had been to pack Ruby and Mary
Jane off to bed with a sound rating. Parson
Babbage had descended also, carrying a heavy
cane (the very same with which he broke
the head of a Radical agitator in the bar
of the "Jolly Pilchards," to the mild scandal
of the diocese), and had routed the rest of
the women and chastised the drunken. The
parson was a remarkable man, and looked
it, just now, in spite of the red handkerchief that bound his hat down over his
ears.

"Nothing alive there—eh?"

Young Zeb, with a glass at his left eye,
answered—

"Nothin' left but a frame o' ribs, sir, an'
the foremast hangin' over, so far as I can see;
but 'tis all a raffle o' spars and riggin' close
under her side. I'll tell 'ee better when this
wave goes by."

But the next instant he took down the glass,
with a whitened face, and handed it to the
parson.

The parson looked too. "Terrible!—

terrible!" he said, very slowly, and passed it on to Farmer Tresidder.

"What is it? Where be I to look? Aw, pore chaps—pore chaps! Man alive—but there's one movin'!"

Zeb snatched the glass.

"'Pon the riggin', Zeb, just under her lee! I saw en move—a black-headed chap, in a red shirt——"

"Right, Farmer—he's clingin', too, not lashed." Zeb gave a long look. "Darned if I won't!" he said. "Cast over them corks, Sim Udy! How much rope have 'ee got, Jim?" He began to strip as he spoke.

"Lashins," answered Jim Lewarne.

"Splice it up, then, an' hitch a dozen corks along it."

"Zeb, Zeb!" cried his father, "What be 'bout?"

"Swimmin'," answered Zeb, who by this time had unlaced his boots.

"The notion! Look here, friends—take a look at the bufflehead! Not three months back his mother's brother goes dead an' leaves

en a legacy, 'pon which he sets up as jowter—
han'some painted cart, tidy little mare, an' all
complete, besides a bravish sum laid by. A
man of substance, sirs—a life o' much price, as
you may say. Aw, Zeb, my son, 'tis hard to
lose 'ee, but 'tis harder still now you're in such
a very fair way o' business!"

"Hold thy clack, father, an' tie thicky knot,
so's it won't slip."

"Shan't. I've a-took boundless pains wi'
thee, my son, from thy birth up: hours I've
a-spent curin' thy prepensities wi' the strap—
ay, hours. D'ee think I raised 'ee up so carefully to chuck thyself away 'pon a come-by-
chance furriner? No, I didn'; an' I'll see
thee jiggered afore I ties 'ee up. Pa'son
Babbage——"

"Ye dundering old shammick!" broke in
the parson, driving the ferule of his cane deep in
the sand, "be content to have begotten a fool,
and thank heaven and his mother he's a gamey
fool."

"Thank'ee, Pa'son," said Young Zeb, turning his head as Jim Lewarne fastened the belt of

corks under his armpits. "Now the line—not too tight round the waist, an' pay out steady. You, Jim, look to this. R-r-r—mortal cold water, friends!" He stood for a moment, clenching his teeth—a fine figure of a youth for all to see. Then, shouting for plenty of line, he ran twenty yards down the beach and leapt in on the top of a tumbling breaker.

"When a man's old," muttered the parson, half to himself, "he may yet thank God for what he sees, sometimes. Hey, Farmer! I wish I was a married man and had a girl good enough for that naked young hero."

"Ruby an' he'll make a han'some pair."

"Ay, I dare say: only I wasn't thinking o' *her*. How's the fellow out yonder?"

The man on the wreck was still clinging, drenched twice or thrice in the half-minute and hidden from sight, but always emerging. He sat astride of the dangling foremast, and had wound tightly round his wrist the end of a rope that hung over the bows. If the rope gave, or the mast worked clear of the tangle that held it and floated off, he was a dead man. He hardly fought at all, and though they shouted at the top of their lungs, seemed to take no notice— only moved feebly, once or twice, to get a firmer seat.

Zeb also could only be descried at intervals, his head appearing, now and again, like a cork on the top of a billow. But the last of the ebb was helping him, and Jim Lewarne, himself at times neck-high in the surf, continued to pay out the line slowly. In fact, the feat was less dangerous than it seemed to the spectators. A few hours before, it was impossible ; but by this there was little more than a heavy swell after the first twenty yards of surf. Zeb's chief difficulty would be to catch a grip or footing on the reef where the sea again grew broken, and his fore-most dread lest cramp should seize him in the bitterly cold water. Rising on the swell, he could spy the seaman tossing and sinking on the mast just ahead.

As it happened, he was spared the main peril of the reef, for in fifty more strokes he found himself plunging down into a smooth trough of water with the mast directly beneath. As he shot down, the mast rose to him, he flung his arms out over it, and was swept up, clutching it, to the summit of the next swell.

Oddly enough, his first thought, as he hung there, was not for the man he had come to save, but for that which had turned him pale when first he glanced through the telescope. The fore-mast across which he lay was complete almost to the royal-mast, though the yards were gone; and to his left, just above the battered fore-top, five men were lashed, dead and drowned. Most of them had their eyes wide open, and seemed to stare at Zeb and wriggle about in the stir of the sea as if they lived. Spent and wretched as he was, it lifted his hair. He almost called out to them at first, and then he dragged his gaze off them, and turned it to the right. The survivor still clung here, and Zeb—who had been vaguely wondering how on earth he contrived to keep his seat and yet hold on by the rope without being torn limb from limb—now discovered this end of the mast to be so tightly jammed and tangled against the wreck as practically to be immovable. The man's face was about as scaring as the

corpses'; for, catching sight of Zeb, he betrayed
no surprise, but only looked back wistfully over
his left shoulder, while his blue lips worked
without sound.　At least, Zeb heard none.

He waited while they plunged again and
emerged, and then, drawing breath, began to pull
himself along towards the stranger.　They had
seen his success from the beach, and Jim
Lewarne, with plenty of line yet to spare, waited
for the next move.　Zeb worked along till he
could touch the man's thigh.

"Keep your knee stiddy," he called out;
"I'm goin' to grip hold o't."

For answer, the stranger only kicked out
with his foot, as a pettish child might, and
almost thrust him from his hold.

"Look'ee here : no doubt you'm 'mazed, but
that's a curst foolish trick, all the same.　Be
that tangle fast, you'm holding by?"

The man made no sign of comprehension.

"Best not trust to't, I reckon," muttered
Zeb: "must get past en an' make fast round a
rib.　Ah! would 'ee, ye varment?"

For, once more, the stranger had tried to

thrust him off; and a struggle followed, which ended in Zeb's getting by and gripping the mast again between him and the wreck.

"Now list to me," he shouted, pulling himself up and flinging a leg over the mast: "ingratitood's worse than witchcraft. Sit ye there an' inwardly digest that sayin', while I saves your life."

He untied the line about his waist, then, watching his chance, snatched the rope out of the other's hand, threw his weight upon it, and swung in towards the vessel's ribs till he touched one, caught, and passed the line around it, high up, with a quick double half-hitch. Running a hand down the line, he dropped back upon the mast. The stranger regarded him with a curious stare, and at last found his voice.

"You seem powerfully set on saving me."

His teeth chattered as he spoke, and his face was pinched and hollow-eyed from cold and exposure. But he was handsome, for all that— a fellow not much older than Zeb, lean and strongly made. His voice had a cultivated ring.

"Yes," answered Zeb, as, with one hand on

the line that now connected the wreck with the shore, he sat down astride the mast facing him; "I reckon I'll do't."

"Unlucky, isn't it?"

"What?"

"To save a man from drowning."

"Maybe. Untie these corks from my chest, and let me slip 'em round yourn. How your fingers do shake, to be sure!"

"I call you to witness," said the other, with a shiver, "you are saving me on your own responsibility."

"Can 'ee swim?"

"I could yesterday."

"Then you can now, wi' a belt o' corks an' me to help. Keep a hand on the line an' pull yoursel' along. Tide's runnin' again by now. When you'm tired, hold fast by the rope an' sing out to me. Stop; let me chafe your legs a bit, for how you've lasted out as you have is more than I know."

"I was on the foretop most of the night. Those fools——" he broke off to nod at the corpses.

"They'm dead," put in Zeb, curtly.

"They lashed themselves, thinking the fore-mast would stand till daylight. I climbed down half an hour before it went. I tell you what, though; my legs are too cramped to move. If you want to save me you must carry me."

"I was thinkin' the same. Well, come along; for tho' I don't like the cut o' your jib, you'm a terrible handsome chap, and as clean-built as ever I see. Now then, one arm round my neck and t'other on the line, but don't bear too hard on it, for I doubt 'tis weakish. Bless the Lord, the tide's running."

So they began their journey. Zeb had taken barely a dozen strokes when the other groaned and began to hang more heavily on his neck. But he fought on, though very soon the struggle became a blind and horrible nightmare to him. The arm seemed to creep round his throat and strangle him, and the blackness of a great night came down over his eyes. Still he struck out, and, oddly enough, found himself calling to his comrade to hold tight.

When Sim Udy and Elias Sweetland dashed

in from the shore and swam to the rescue, they found the pair clinging to the line, and at a standstill. And when the four were helped through the breakers to firm earth, Zeb tottered two steps forward and dropped in a swoon, burying his face in the sand.

"He's not as strong as I," muttered the stranger, staring at Parson Babbage in a dazed, uncertain fashion, and uttering the words as if they had no connection with his thoughts. "I'm afraid—sir—I've broken—his heart."

And with that he, too, fainted, into the Parson's arms.

"Better carry the both up to Sheba," said Farmer Tresidder.

Ruby lay still abed when Mary Jane, who had been moving about the kitchen, sleepy-eyed, getting ready the breakfast, dashed up-stairs with the news that two dead men had been taken off the wreck and were even now being brought into the yard.

"You coarse girl," she exclaimed, "to frighten me with such horrors!"

"Oh, very well," answered Mary Jane, who was in a rebellious mood, "then I'm goin' down to peep; for there's a kind o' what-I-can't-tell-'ee about dead men that's very enticin', tho' it do make you feel all-overish."

By and by she came back panting, to find Ruby already dressed.

"Aw, Miss Ruby, dreadful news I ha' to tell, tho' joyous in a way. Would 'ee mind catchin' hold o' the bed-post to give yoursel' fortitude? Now let me cast about how to break it softly. First, then, you must know he's not dead at all——"

"Who is not?"

"Your allotted husband, miss — Mister Zeb."

"Why, who in the world said he was?"

"But they took en up for dead, miss—for he'd a-swum out to the wreck, an' then he'd a-swum back with a man 'pon his back—an' touchin' shore, he fell downward in a swound, marvellous like to death for all to behold. So they brought en up here, 'long wi' the chap he'd a-saved, an' dressed en i' the spare room blankets, an' gave en

clane sperrits to drink, an' lo! he came to; an' in
a minnit, lo! agen he went off; an'———"

Ruby, by this time, was half-way down the
stairs. Running to the kitchen door she flung it
open, calling "Zeb! Zeb!"

But Young Zeb had fainted for the third time,
and while others of the group merely lifted their
heads at her entrance, the old crowder strode
towards her with some amount of sternness on
his face.

"Kape off my son!" he shouted. "Kape
off my son Zebedee, and go up-stairs agen to
your prayers; for this be all your work, in a
way—you gay good-for-nuthin'!"

"Indeed, Mr. Minards," retorted Ruby, firing
up under this extravagant charge and bridling,
"pray remember whose roof you're under, with
your low language."

"Begad," interposed a strange voice, "but
that's the spirit for me, and the mouth to utter
it!"

Ruby, turning, met a pair of luminous eyes
gazing on her with bold admiration. The eyes
were set in a cadaverous, but handsome, face;

and the face belonged to the stranger, who had recovered of his swoon, and was now stretched on the settle beside the fire.

"I don't know who you may be, sir, but——"

"You are kind enough to excuse my rising to introduce myself. My name is Zebedee Minards."

CHAPTER IV.

YOUNG ZEB FETCHES A CHEST OF DRAWERS.

THE parish of Ruan Lanihale is bounded on the
west by Porthlooe, a fishing town of fifteen
hundred inhabitants or less, that blocks the sea-
ward exit of a narrow coombe. A little stream
tumbles down this coombe towards the "Hauen,"
divides the folk into parishioners of Lanihale and
Landaviddy, and receives impartially the fish
offal of both. There is a good deal of this offal,
especially during pilchard time, and the townsfolk live on their first storeys, using the lower
floors as fish cellars, or "pallaces." But even
while the nose most abhors, the eye is delighted
by jumbled houses, crazy stairways leading to
green doors, a group of children dabbling in the
mud at low tide, a congregation of white gulls, a
line of fishing boats below the quay where the
men lounge and whistle and the barked nets
hang to dry, and, beyond all, the shorn outline

of two cliffs with a wedge of sea and sky between.

Mr. Zebedee Minards the elder dwelt on the eastern or Lanihale side of the stream, and a good way back from the Hauen, beside the road that winds inland up the coombe. Twenty yards of garden divided his cottage door from the road, and prevented the inmates from breaking their necks as they stepped over its threshold. Even as it was, Old Zeb had acquired a habit of singing out " Ware heads ! " to the wayfarers whenever he chanced to drop a rotund object on his estate ; and if any small article were missing indoors, would descend at once to the highway with the cheerful assurance, based on repeated success, of finding it somewhere below.

Over and above its recurrent crop of potatoes and flatpoll cabbages, this precipitous garden depended for permanent interest on a collection of marine curiosities, all eloquent of disaster to shipping. To begin with, a colossal and highly varnished Cherokee, once the figure-head of a West Indiaman, stood sentry by the gate and hung forward over the road, to the discomfiture

E 2

of unwarned and absent-minded bagmen. The path to the door was guarded by a low fence of split-bamboo baskets that had once contained sugar from Batavia; a coffee bag from the wreck of a Dutch barque served for door-mat; a rum-cask with a history caught rain-water from the eaves; and a lapdog's pagoda—a dainty affair, striped in scarlet and yellow, the jetsom of some passenger ship—had been deftly adapted by Old Zeb, and stood in line with three straw bee-skips under the eastern wall.

The next day but one after Christmas dawned deliciously in Porthlooe, bright with virginal sunshine, and made tender by the breath of the Gulf Stream. Uncle Issy, passing up the road at nine o'clock, halted by the Cherokee to pass a word with its proprietor, who presented the very antipodes of a bird's-eye view, as he knocked about the crumbling clods with his visgy at the top of the slope.

"Mornin', Old Zeb; how be 'ee, this dellicate day?"

"Brave, thankee, Uncle."

"An' how's Coden Rachel?"

" She's charmin', thankee."

" Comely weather, comely weather; the gulls be comin' back down the coombe, I see."

" I be jealous about its lastin'; for 'tis over-rathe for the time o' year. Terrible topsy-turvy the seasons begin to run, in my old age. Here's May in Janewarry; an' 'gainst May, comes th' east wind breakin' the ships o' Tarshish."

" Now, what an instructive chap you be to convarse with, I do declare! Darned if I didn' stand here two minnits, gazin' up at the seat o' your small-clothes, tryin' to think 'pon what I wanted to say; for I'd a notion that I wanted to speak, cruel bad, but cudn' lay hand on't. So at last I takes heart an' says ' Mornin',' I says, beginnin' i' that very common way an' hopin' 'twould come. An' round you whips wi' ' ships o' Tarshish' pon your tongue; an' henceforth 'tis all Q's an' A's, like a cattykism."

" Well, now you say so, I *did* notice, when I turned round, that you was lookin' no better than a fool, so to speak. But what's the notion? "

" 'Tis a question I've a-been daggin' to ax'ee ever since it woke me up in the night to spekilate thereon. For I felt it very curious there shud be three Zebedee Minardses i' this parish a-drawin' separate breath at the same time."

" Iss, 'tis an out-o'-the-way fact."

" A stirrin' age, when such things befall! If you'd a-told me, a week agone, that I should live to see the like, I'd ha' called 'ee a liar; an' yet here I be a-talkin' away, an' there you be a-listenin', an' here be the old world a-spinnin' us round as in bygone times——"

" Iss, iss—but what's the question?"

"—All the same when that furriner chap looks up in Tresidder's kitchen an' says ' My name is Zebedee Minards,' you might ha' blown me down wi' a puff; an' says I to mysel', wakin' up last night an' thinkin'—' I'll ax a question of Old Zeb when I sees en, blest if I don't.' "

" Then why in thunder don't 'ee make haste an' do it?"

Uncle Issy, after revolving the question for another fifteen seconds, produced it in this attractive form—

" Old Zeb, bein' called Zeb, why did 'ee call Young Zeb, Zeb?"

Old Zeb ceased to knock the clods about, descended the path, and leaning on his visgy began to contemplate the opposite slope of the coombe, as if the answer were written, in letters hard to decipher, along the hill-side.

" Well, now," he began, after opening his mouth twice and shutting it without sound, "folks may say what they like o' your wits, Uncle, an' talk o' your looks bein' against 'ee, as they do; but you've a-put a twister, this time, an' no mistake."

" I reckoned it a banger," said the old man, complacently.

" Iss. But I had my reasons all the same."

" To be sure you had. But rabbet me if I can guess what they were."

" I'll tell 'ee. You see when Zeb was born, an' the time runnin' on for his christ'nin', Rachel an' me puzzled for days what to call en. At last I said, ' Look 'ere, I tell 'ee what : you shut your eyes an' open the Bible, anyhow, an' I'll shut mine an' take a dive wi' my finger, an' we'll call en by the nearest name I hits on.' So we did. When we tuk en to church, tho', there was a

pretty shape. 'Name this cheeld,' says Pa'son
Babbage. 'Selah,' says I, that bein' the word
we'd settled. 'Selah?' says he: 'pack o' stuff!
that ain't no manner o' name. You might so
well call en Amen.' So bein' hurried in mind,
what wi' the cheeld kickin', an' the water
tricklin' off the pa'son's forefinger, an' the sacred
natur' of the deed, I cudn' think 'pon no name
but my own; an' Zeb he was christened."

"Deary me," commented Uncle Issy, "that's
a very life-like history. The wonder is, the
self-same fix don't happen at more christ'nin's,
'tis so very life-like."

A silence followed, full of thought. It was
cut short by the rattle of wheels coming down
the road, and Young Zeb's grey mare hove in
sight, with Young Zeb's green cart, and Young
Zeb himself standing up in it, wide-legged. He
wore a colour as fresh as on Christmas morning,
and seemed none the worse for his adventure.

"Hello!" he called, pulling up the mare;
"'mornin', Uncle Issy—'mornin', father."

"Same to you, my son. Whither away?—
as the man said once."

"Aye, whither away?" chimed Uncle Issy; "for the pilchards be all gone up Channel these two months."

"To Liskeard, for a chest-o'-drawers."

Young Zeb, to be ready for married life, had taken a house for himself—a neat cottage with a yard and stable, farther up the coombe. But stress of business had interfered with the furnishing until quite lately.

"Rale meogginy, I suppose, as befits a proud tradesman."

"No: painted, but wi' the twiddles put in so artfully you'd think 'twas rale. So, as 'tis a fine day, I'm drivin' in to Mister Pennyway's shop o' purpose to fetch it afore it be snapped up, for 'tis a captivatin' article. I'll be back by six, tho', i' time to get into my clothes an' grease my hair for the courant, up to Sheba."

"Zeb," said his father, abruptly, "'tis a grand match you'm makin', an' you may call me a nincom, but I wish ye wasn'."

"'Tis lookin' high," put in Uncle Issy.

"A cat may look at a king, if he's got his eyes about en," Old Zeb went on, "let alone a legacy an' a green cart. 'Tain't that: 'tis the maid."

"How's mother?" asked the young man, to shift the conversation.

"Hugly, my son. Hi! Rachel!" he shouted, turning his head towards the cottage; and then went on, dropping his voice, "As between nay-bours, I'm fain to say she don't shine this mornin'. Hi, mother! here's Zebedee waitin' to pay his respects."

Mrs. Minards appeared on the cottage thres-hold, with a blue check duster round her head— a tall, angular woman, of severe deportment. Her husband's bulletin, it is fair to say, had reference rather to her temper than to her personal attractions.

"Be the Frenchmen landed?" she inquired, sharply.

"Why, no; nor yet likely to."

"Then why be I called out i' the midst o' my clanin'? What came I out for to see? Was it to pass the time o' day wi' an aged shaken-by-the-wind kind o' loiterer they name Uncle Issy?"

Apparently it was not, for Uncle Issy by this time was twenty yards up the road, and still fleeing, with his head bent and shoulders extravagantly arched, as if under a smart shower.

" I thought I'd like to see you, mother," said Young Zeb.

" Well, now you've done it."

" Best be goin', I reckon, my son," whispered Old Zeb.

" I be much the same to look at," announced the voice above, "as afore your legacy came. 'Tis only up to Sheba that faces ha' grown kindlier."

Young Zeb touched up his mare a trifle savagely.

" Well, so long, my son ! See 'ee up to Sheba this evenin', if all's well."

The old man turned back to his work, while Young Zeb rattled on in an ill humour. He had the prettiest sweetheart and the richest in Lani-hale parish, and nobody said a good word for her. He tried to think of her as a wronged angel, and grew angry with himself on finding the effort hard to sustain. Moreover, he felt uneasy about the stranger. Fate must be intending mischief, he fancied, when it led him to rescue a man who so strangely happened to bear his own name. The fellow, too, was still at Sheba, being nursed back to strength; and Zeb didn't like it. In spite of the day, and the merry breath of it that blew from the sea upon his right cheek, black care dogged him all the way up the long hill that led out of Porthlooe, and clung to the tail-board of his green cart as he jolted down again towards Ruan Cove.

After passing the Cove-head, Young Zeb pulled up the mare, and was taken with a fit of thoughtfulness, glancing up towards Sheba farm, and then along the high-road, as if uncertain. The mare settled the question after a minute, by turning into the lane, and Zeb let her have her way.

"Where's Miss Ruby?" he asked, driving into the town-place, and coming on Mary Jane, who was filling a pig's-bucket by the back door.

"Gone up to Parc Dew 'long wi' maister an'

the very man I seed i' my tay-cup, a week come Friday."

" H'm."

" Iss, fay; an' a great long-legged stranger he was. So I stuck en 'pon my fist an' gave en a scat. 'To-day,' says I, but he didn' budge. 'To-morrow,' I says, an' gave en another; and then 'Nex' day;' and t' third time he flew. 'Shall have a sweet'eart, Sunday, praise the Lord,' thinks I; 'wonder who 'tis? Anyway, 'tis a comfort he'll be high 'pon his pins, like Nanny Painter's hens, for mine be all the purgy-bustious shape just now.' Well, Sunday night he came to Raney Rock, an' Monday mornin' to Sheba farm; and no thanks to you that brought en, for not a single dare-to-deny-me glance has he cast *this* way."

" Which way, then ? "

" 'Can't stay to causey, Master Zeb, wi' all the best horn-handled knives to be took out o' blue-butter 'gainst this evenin's courant. Besides, you called me a liar last week."

" So you be. But I'll believe 'ee this time."

" Well, I'll tell 'ee this much—for you look

a very handsome jowter i' that new cart. If I were you, I'd be careful that gay furriner *didn' steal more'n my name.*"

Meantime, a group of four was standing in the middle of Parc Dew, the twenty-acred field behind the farmstead. The stranger, dressed in a blue jersey and outfit of Farmer Tresidder's, that made up in boots for its shortcomings elsewhere, was addressing the farmer, Ruby, and Jim Lewarne, who heard him with lively attention. In his right hand he held a walking-stick armed with a spud, for uprooting thistles ; and in his left a cake of dark soil, half stone, half mud. His manner was earnest.

". . . . I see," he was saying, " that I don't convince you ; and it's only for your own sakes I insist on convincing you. You'll grant me that, I suppose. To-morrow, or the next day, I go ; and the chances are that we never meet again in this world. But 'twould be a pleasant thought to carry off to the ends of the earth that you, my benefactors, were living in wealth, enriched (if I may say it without presumption)

by a chance word of mine. I tell you I know
something of these matters——"

"I thought you'd passed your days priva-
teerin'," put in Jim Lewarne, who was the only
hostile listener, perhaps because he saw no
chance of sharing in the promised wealth.

"Jim, hold your tongue!" snapped Ruby.

"I ask you," went on the stranger, without
deigning to answer, "I ask you if it does not
look like Providence? Here have you been for
years, dwelling amid wealth of which you never
dreamed. A ship is wrecked close to your
doors, and of all her crew the one man saved is,
perhaps, the one man who could enlighten you.
You feed him, clothe him, nurse him. As soon
as he can crawl about, he picks a walking-stick
out of half-a-dozen or more in the hall, and goes
out with you to take a look at the farm. On
his way he notes many things. He sees (you'll
excuse me, Farmer, but I can't help it) that
you're all behind the world, and the land is
yielding less than half of what it ought. Have
you ever seen a book by Lord Dundonald
on the connection between Agriculture and

Chemistry? No? I thought not. Do you know of any manure better than the ore-weed you gather down at the Cove? Or the plan of malting grain to feed your cattle on through the winter? Or the respective merits of oxen and horses as beasts of draught? But these matters, though the life and soul of modern husbandry, are as nothing to this lump in my hand. What do you call the field we're now standing in?"

"Parc Dew."

"Exactly—the 'black field,' or the 'field of black soil': the very name should have told you. But you lay it down in grass, and but for the chance of this spud and a lucky thistle, I might have walked over it a score of times without guessing its secret. Man alive, it's red gold I have here—-red, wicked, damnable, delicious gold—the root of all evil and of most joys."

"If you lie, you lie enticingly, young man."

"By gold, I mean stuff that shall make gold for you. There is ore here, but what ore exactly I can't tell till I've streamed it: lead, I fancy, with a trace of silver—wealth for you, certainly; and in what quantity you shall find out——"

At this juncture a voice was heard calling over the hedge, at the bottom of the field. It came from Young Zeb, the upper part of whose person, as he stood up in his cart, was just visible between two tamarisk bushes.

" Ru-b-y-y-y ! "

" Drat the chap ! " exclaimed Ruby's father, wheeling round sharply. " What d'ye wa-a-a-nt ? " he yelled back.

" Come to know 'bout that chest o' dra-w-w-ers ! "

" Then come 'long round by th' ga-a-ate ! "

" Can't sta-a-ay ! Want to know, as I'm drivin' to Liskeard, if Ruby thinks nine-an'-six too mu-u-ch, as the twiddles be so very cle-v-ver ! "

" How ridiculous ! " muttered the stranger, just loud enough for Ruby to hear. " Who is this absurd person ? "

Jim Lewarne answered—" A low-lived chap, mister, as saved your skin awhile back."

" Dear, dear—how unpardonable of me ! I

F

hadn't the least idea at this distance. Excuse
me, I must go and thank him at once."

He moved towards the hedge with a brisk
step that seemed to cost him some pain. The
others followed, a pace or two behind.

" You'll not mind my interruptin', Farmer,"
continued Young Zeb, " but 'tis time Ruby
made her mind up, for Mister Pennyway
won't take a stiver less. 'Mornin', Ruby, my
dear."

" And you'll forgive me if I also interrupt,"
put in the stranger, with the pleasantest smile,
" but it is time I thanked the friend who saved
my life on Monday morning. I would come
round and shake hands if only I could see the
gate."

" Don't 'ee mention it," replied Zeb, blush-
ing hotly. " I'm glad to mark ye lookin' so
brave a'ready. Well, what d'ye say, Ruby ? "

" I say ' please yoursel'.' "

For of the two men standing before Ruby
(she did not count her father and Jim Lewarne),
the stranger, with his bold features and easy
conciliating carriage, had the advantage. It is

probable that he knew it, and threw a touch of acting into his silence as Zeb cut him short.

"That's a fair speech," replied Zeb. "Iss, turn it how you will, the words be winnin' enow. But be danged, my dear, if I wudn' as lief you said, 'Go to blazes!'"

"Fact is, my son," said Farmer Tresidder, candidly, "you'm good but untimely, like kissin' the wrong maid. This here surpassin' young friend o' mine was speech-makin' after a pleasant fashion in our ears when you began to bawl——"

"Then you don't want to hear about the chest o' drawers?" interrupted Zeb in dudgeon, with a glance at Ruby, who pretended not to see it.

"Well, no. To tell 'ee the slap-bang truth, I don't care if I see no trace of 'ee till the dancin' begins to commence to-night."

"Then good-day t' ye, friends," answered Young Zeb, and turned the mare. "Cl'k, Jessamy!" He rattled away down the lane.

"What an admirable youth!" murmured the stranger, falling back a pace and gazing after the back of Zeb's head as it passed down the line of the hedge. "What a messenger! He seems eaten up with desire to get you a chest of drawers that shall be wholly satisfying. But why do you allow him to call you 'my dear'?"

"Because, I suppose, that's what I am," answered Ruby; "because I'm goin' to marry him within the month."

"*Wh-e-e-w!*"

But, as a matter of fact, the stranger had known before asking.

CHAPTER V.

IT was close upon midnight, and in the big parlour at Sheba the courant, having run through its normal stages of high punctilio, artificial ease, zest, profuse perspiration, and supper, had reached the exact point when Modesty Prowse could be surprised under the kissing-bush, and Old Zeb wiped his spectacles, thrust his chair back, and pushed out his elbows to make sure of room for the rendering of "Scarlet's my Colour." These were tokens to be trusted by an observer who might go astray in taking any chance guest as a standard of the average conviviality. Mr. and Mrs. Jim Lewarne, for example, were accustomed on such occasions to represent the van and rear-guard respectively in the march of gaiety; and in this instance Jim had already imbibed too much hot "shenachrum," while his wife, still

in the stage of artificial ease, and wearing a lace
cap, which was none the less dignified for
having been smuggled, was perpending what
to say when she should get him home. The
dancers, pale and dusty, leant back in rows
against the wall, and with their handkerchiefs
went through the motions of fanning or polish-
ing, according to sex. In their midst circulated
Farmer Tresidder, with a three-handled mug of
shenachrum, hot from the embers, and furred
with wood-ash.

"Take an' drink, thirsty souls. Niver do I
mind the Letterpooch so footed i' my born
days."

"'Twas conspirator—very conspirator," assented Old Zeb, screwing up his A string a
trifle, and turning *con spirito* into a dark
saying.

"What's that?"

"Greek for elbow-grease. Phew!" He
rubbed his fore-finger round between neck and
shirt-collar. "I be vady as the inside of a
winder."

"Such a man as you be to sweat, crowder!"

exclaimed Calvin Oke. "Set you to play six-eight time an' 'tis beads right away."

"A slice o' saffern-cake, crowder, to stay ye. Don't say no. Hi, Mary Jane!"

"Thank 'ee, Farmer. A man might say you was in sperrits to-night, makin' so bold."

"I be; I be."

"Might a man ax wherefore, beyond the nat'ral hail-fellow-well-met of the season?"

"You may, an' yet you mayn't," answered the host, passing on with the mug.

"Uncle Issy," asked Jim Lewarne, lurching up, "I durstn' g-glint over my shoulder—but wud 'ee mind tellin' me if th' old woman's lookin' this way—afore I squench my thirst?"

"Iss, she be."

Jim groaned. "Then wud 'ee mind a-hof-ferin' me a taste out o' your pannikin? an' I'll make b'lieve to say 'Norronany 'count.' Amazin' 'ot t' night," he added, tilting back on his heels, and then dipping forward with a vague smile.

Uncle Issy did as he was required, and the henpecked one played his part of the comedy with elaborate slyness. " I don't like that strange chap," he announced, irrelevantly.

"Nor I nuther," agreed Elias Sweetland, "tho' to be sure, I've a-kept my eye 'pon en, an' the wonders he accomplishes in an old pair o' Tresidder's high-lows must be seen to be believed. But that's no call for Ruby's dancin' wi' he a'most so much as wi' her proper man."

"The gel's takin' her fling afore wedlock. I heard Sarah Ann Nanjulian, just now, sayin' she ought to be clawed."

"A jealous woman is a scourge shaken to an' fro," said Old Zeb; " but I've a mind, friends, to strike up ' Randy my dandy,' for that son o' mine is lookin' blacker than the horned man, an' may be 'twill comfort 'en to dance afore the public eye; for there's none can take his wind in a hornpipe."

In fact, it was high time that somebody comforted Young Zeb, for his heart was hot. He had brought home the chest of drawers in his cart, and spent an hour fixing on the best position for it in the bedroom, before dressing for the dance. Also he had purchased, in Mr.

Pennyway's shop, an armchair, in the worst taste, to be a pleasant surprise for Ruby when the happy day came for installing her. Finding he had still twenty minutes to spare after giving the last twitch to his neckerchief, and the last brush to his anointed locks, he had sat down facing this chair, and had striven to imagine her in it, darning his stockings. Zeb was not, as a rule, imaginative, but love drew this delicious picture for him. He picked up his hat, and set out for Sheba in the best of tempers.

But at Sheba all had gone badly. Ruby's frock of white muslin and Ruby's small sandal shoes were bewitching, but Ruby's mood passed his intelligence. It was true she gave him half the dances, but then she gave the other half to that accursed stranger, and the stranger had all her smiles, which was carrying hospitality too far. Not a word had she uttered to Zeb beyond the merest commonplaces; on the purchase of the chest of drawers she had breathed no question; she hung listlessly on his arm, and spoke only of the music, the other girls' frocks, the arrangement of the supper-table. And at supper the stranger had not only sat on the other side of her, but had talked all the time, and on books, a subject entirely uninteresting to Zeb. Worst of all, Ruby had listened. No; the worst of all was a remark of Modesty Prowse's that he chanced to overhear afterwards.

So when the fiddles struck up the air of "Randy my dandy," Zeb, knowing that the company would call upon him, at first felt his heart turn sick with loathing. He glanced across the room at Ruby, who, with heightened colour, was listening to the stranger, and looking up at his handsome face. Already one or two voices were calling "Zeb!" "Young Zeb for a hornpipe!" "Now then, Young Zeb!"

He had a mind to refuse. For years after he remembered every small detail of the room as he looked down it and then across to Ruby again : the motion of the fiddle-bows; the variegated dresses of the women; the kissing-bush that some tall dancer's head had set swaying from the low rafter; the light of a sconce gleaming on Tresidder's bald scalp. Years after, he could recall the exact poise of Ruby's

head as she answered some question of her companion. The stranger left her, and strolled
slowly down the room to the fireplace, when he
faced round, throwing an arm negligently along
the mantel-shelf, and leant with legs crossed,
waiting.

Then Young Zeb made up his mind, and
stepped out into the middle of the floor. The
musicians were sawing with might and main at
high speed. He crossed his arms, and, fixing
his eyes on the stranger's, began the hornpipe.

When it ceased, he had danced his best. It
was only when the applause broke out that he
knew he had fastened, from start to finish, on
the man by the fireplace a pair of eyes blazing
with hate. The other had stared back quietly,
as if he noted only the performance. As the
music ended sharply with the click of Young
Zeb's two heels, the stranger bent, took up a
pair of tongs, and rearranged the fire before
lifting his head.

"Yes," he said, slowly, but in tones that
were extremely distinct as the clapping died
away, "that was wonderfully danced. In some

ways I should almost say you were inspired.
A slight want of airiness in the double-shuffle,
perhaps——"

"Could you do't better?" asked Zeb, sulkily.

"That isn't the fair way to treat criticism,
my friend; but yes—oh, yes, certainly I could
do it better—in your shoes."

"Then try, i' my shoes." And Zeb kicked
them off.

"I've a notion they'll fit me," was all the
stranger answered, dropping on one knee and
beginning to unfasten the cumbrous boots he
had borrowed of Farmer Tresidder.

Indeed, the curious likeness in build of these
two men—a likeness accentuated, rather than
slurred, by their contrast in colour and face, was
now seen to extend even to their feet. When
the stranger stood up at length in Zeb's shoes,
they fitted him to a nicety, the broad steel
buckles lying comfortably over the instep, the
back of the uppers closing round the hollow
of his ankle like a skin.

Young Zeb, by this, had crossed shoeless to
the fireplace, and now stood in the position

lately occupied by his rival: only, whereas the
stranger had lolled easily, Zeb stood squarely,
with his legs wide apart and his hands deep
in his pockets. He had no eyes for the intent
faces around, no ears for their whispering, nor
for the preliminary scrape of the instruments;
but stood like an image, with the firelight
flickering out between his calves, and watched
the other man grimly.

"Ready?" asked his father's voice. "Then
one—two—three, an' let fly!"

The fiddle-bows hung for an instant on the
first note, and in a twinkling scampered along into
"Randy my dandy." As the quick air caught
at the listeners' pulses, the stranger crossed his
arms, drew his right heel up along the inner
side of his left ankle, and with a light nod
towards the chimney-place began.

To the casual eye there was for awhile
little to choose between the two dancers, the
stranger's style being accurate, restrained, even
a trifle dull. But of all the onlookers, Zeb
knew best what hornpipe-dancing really was;
and knew surely, after the first dozen steps, that

he was going to be mastered. So far, the performance was academic only. Zeb, unacquainted with the word, recognised the fact, and was quite aware of the inspiration—the personal gift —held in reserve to transfigure this precise art in a minute or so, and give it life. He saw the force gathering in the steady rhythmical twinkle of the steel buckles, and heard it speak in the light recurrent tap with which the stranger's heels kissed the floor. It was doubly bitter that he and his enemy alone should know what was coming; trebly bitter that his enemy should be aware that he knew.

The crowder slackened speed for a second, to give warning, and dashed into the heel-and-toe. Zeb caught the light in the dancer's eyes, and still frowning, drew a long breath.

"Faster," nodded the stranger to the musicians' corner.

Then came the moment for which, by this time, Zeb was longing. The stranger rested with heels together while a man might count eight rapidly, and suddenly began a step the like of which none present had ever witnessed.

Above the hips his body swayed steadily, softly, to the measure ; his eyes never took their pleasant smile off Zeb's face, but his feet——

The steel buckles had become two sparkling moths, spinning, poising, darting. They no longer belonged to the man, but had taken separate life : and merely the absolute symmetry of their loops and circles, and the *click-click-click* on boards, regular as ever, told of the art that informed them.

" Faster ! "

They crossed and re-crossed now like small flashes of lightning, or as if the boards were flints giving out a score of sparks at every touch of the man's heel.

" Faster ! "

They seemed suddenly to catch the light out of every sconce, and knead it into a ball of fire, that spun and yet was motionless, in the very middle of the floor, while all the rest of the room grew suddenly dimmed.

Zeb with a gasp drew his eyes away for a second and glanced around. Fiddlers and guests seemed ghostly after the fierce light he had been gazing on. He looked along the pale faces to the place where Ruby stood. She, too, glanced up, and their eyes met.

What he saw fetched a sob from his throat. Then something on the floor caught his attention: something bright, close by his feet.

Between his out-spread legs, as it seemed, a thin streak of silver was creeping along the flooring. He rubbed his eyes, and looked again.

He was straddling across a stream of molten metal.

As Zeb caught sight of this, the stranger twirled, leapt a foot in the air, and came down smartly on the final note, with a click of his heels. The music ceased abruptly.

A storm of clapping broke out, but stopped almost on the instant: for the stranger had flung an arm out towards the hearth-stone.

" A mine—a mine ! "

The white streak ran hissing from the heart of the fire, where a clod of earth rested among the ashen sticks.

" Witchcraft ! " muttered one or two of the guests, peering forward with round eyes.

" Fiddlestick-end! I put the clod there myself. 'Tis *lead !* "

" Lead ? "

" Ay, naybours all," broke in Farmer Tresidder, his bald head bedewed with sweat, "I don't want to abash 'ee, Lord knows ; but 'tis trew as doom that I be a passing well-to-do chap. I shudn' wonder now " — and here he embraced the company with a smile, half pompous and half timid— " I shudn' wonder if ye was to see me trottin' to Parly-ment House in a gilded coach afore Michael-mas—I be so tremenjous rich, by all ac-counts."

" You'll excoose my sayin' it, Farmer," spoke up Old Zeb out of the awed silence that followed, "for doubtless I may be thick o' hearin', but did I, or did I not, catch 'ee alludin' to a windfall o' wealth ? "

" You did."

" You'll excoose me sayin' it, Farmer ; but was it soberly or pleasantly, honest creed or light lips, down-right or random, ' out o' the heart the mouth speaketh ' or wantonly and in

G

round figgers, as it might happen to a man filled with meat and wine ? "

" 'Twas the cold trewth."

" By what slice o' fortune ? "

" By a mine, as you might put it: or, as between man an' man, by a mine o' lead."

" Farmer, you're either a born liar or the darlin' o' luck."

" Aye : I feel it. I feel that overpowerin'ly."

" For my part," put in Mrs. Jim Lewarne, " I've given over follerin' the freaks o' Fortune. They be so very undiscernin'."

And this sentence probably summed up the opinion of the majority.

In the midst of the excitement Young Zeb strode up to the stranger, who stood a little behind the throng.

" Give me back my shoes," he said.

The other kicked them off and looked at him oddly.

" With pleasure. You'll find them a bit worn, I'm afraid."

"I'll chance that. Man, I'm not all sorry, either."

"Hey, why?"

"'Cause they'll not be worn agen, arter this night. Gentleman or devil, whichever you may be, I bain't fit to dance i' the same parish with 'ee—no, nor to tread the shoeleather you've worn."

"By the powers!" cried the stranger suddenly, "two minutes ago I'd have agreed with you. But, looking in your eyes, I'm not so sure of it."

"Of what?"

"That you won't wear the shoes again."

Then Zeb went after Ruby.

"I want to speak a word with 'ee," he said quietly, stepping up to her.

"Where?"

"I' the hall."

"But I can't come, just now."

"But you must."

She followed him out.

"Zeb, what's the matter with you?"

G 2

" Look here "—and he faced round sharply
—" I loved you passing well."

" Well ? " she asked, like a faint echo.

" I saw your eyes, just now. Don't lie."

" I won't."

" That's right. And now listen : if you
marry me, I'll treat 'ee like a span'el dog.
Fetch you shall, an' carry, for my pleasure.
You shall be slave, an' I your taskmaster; an'
the sweetness o' your love shall come by
crushin', like trodden thyme. Shall I suit
you ? "

" I don't think you will."

" Then good-night to you."

" Good-night, Zeb. I don't fancy you'll
suit me ; but I'm not so sure as before you
began to speak."

There was no answer to this but the
slamming of the front door.

" At half-past seven that morning, Parson
Babbage, who had risen early, after his wont,
was standing on the Vicarage doorstep to re-
spire the first breath of the pale day, when he

heard the garden gate unlatched and saw Young
Zeb coming up the path.

The young man still wore his festival dress ;
but his best stockings and buckled shoes were
stained and splashed, as from much walking in
miry ways. Also he came unsteadily, and his
face was white as ashes. The parson stared
and asked—

" Young Zeb, have you been drinking ? "

"No."

" Then 'tis trouble, my son, an' I ask your
pardon."

" A man might call it so. I'm come to
forbid my banns."

The elder man cocked his head on one side,
much as a thrush contemplates a worm.

" I smell a wise wit, somewhere. Young
man, who taught you so capital a notion ? "

" Ruby did."

" Pack o' stuff ! Ruby hadn't the—stop a
minute ! 'twas that clever fellow you fetched
ashore, on Monday. Of course—of course !
How came it to slip my mind ? "

Young Zeb turned away ; but the old man

was after him, quick as thought, and had laid a
hand on his shoulder.

" Is it bitter, my son? "

" It is bitter as death, Pa'son."

" My poor lad.   Step in an' break your fast
with me—poor lad, poor lad !   Nay, but you
shall.   There's a bitch pup i' the stables that I
want your judgment on.   Bitter, eh ?   I dessay.
I dessay.   I'm thinking of walking her—lemon
spot on the left ear—Rattler strain, of course.
Dear me, this makes six generations I can count
back that spot—an' game every one.   Step in,
poor lad, step in : she's a picture."

CHAPTER VI.

SIEGE IS LAID TO RUBY.

THE sun was higher by some hours—high enough to be streaming brightly over the wall into the courtlage at Sheba—when Ruby awoke from a dreamless sleep. As she lifted her head from the pillow and felt the fatigue of last night yet in her limbs, she was aware also of a rich tenor voice uplifted beneath her window. Air and words were strange to her, and the voice had little in common with the world as she knew it. Its exile on that coast was almost pathetic, and it dwelt on the notes with a feeling of a warmer land.

> " *O south be north—*
> *O sun be shady—*
> *Until my lady*
> *Shall issue forth :*
> *Till her own mouth*
> *Bid sun uncertain*

> *To draw his curtain,*
> *Bid south be south."*

She stole out of bed and went on tiptoe to
the window, where she drew the blind an inch
aside.   The stranger's footstep had ceased to
crunch the gravel, and he stood now just beneath
her, before the monthly-rose bush.   Throughout
the winter a blossom or two lingered in that
sheltered corner ; and he had drawn the nearest
down to smell at it.

> " *O heart, her rose,*
> *I cannot ease thee*
> *Till she release thee*
> *And bid unclose.*
> *So, till day come*
> *And she be risen,*
> *Rest, rose, in prison*
> *And heart be dumb !* "

He snapped the stem and passed on, whistling
the air of his ditty, and twirling the rose between
finger and thumb.

" Men are all ninnies," Ruby decided as she
dropped the blind ; " and I thank the fates that

framed me female and priced me high. Heigho!
but it's a difficult world for women. Either a
man thinks you an angel, and then you know
him for a fool, or he sees through you and won't
marry you for worlds. If *we* behaved like that,
men would fare badly, I reckon. Zeb loved me
till the very moment I began to respect him:
then he left off. If this one . . . I like his
cool way of plucking my roses, though. Zeb
would have waited and wanted, till the flower
dropped."

She spent longer than usual over her dressing: so that when she appeared in the parlour
the two men were already seated at breakfast.
The room still bore traces of last night's frolic.
The uncarpeted boards gleamed as the guests'
feet had polished them; and upon the very spot
where the stranger had danced now stood the
breakfast-table, piled with broken meats. This
alone of all the heavier pieces of furniture had
been restored to its place. As Ruby entered,
the stranger broke off an earnest conversation
he was holding with the farmer, and stood up
to greet her. The rose lay on her plate.

" Who has robbed my rose-bush ? " she asked.

" I am guilty," he answered : " I stole it to give it back ; and, not being mine, 'twas the harder to part with."

" To my mind," broke in Farmer Tresidder, with his mouth full of ham, " the best part o' the feast be the over-plush. Squab pie, muggetty pie, conger pie, sweet giblet pie—such a whack of pies do try a man, to be sure. Likewise junkets an' heavy cake be a responsibility, for if not eaten quick, they perish. But let it be mine to pass my days with a cheek o' pork like the present instance. Ruby, my dear, the young man here wants to lave us."

" Leave us ? " echoed Ruby, pricking her finger deep in the act of pinning the stranger's rose in her bosom.

" You hear, young man. That's the tone o' speech signifyin' ' damn it all ! ' among women. And so say I, wi' all these vittles cryin' out to be ate."

" These brisk days," began the stranger quietly, " are not to be let slip. I have no wife, no kin, no friends, no fortune — or only the pound or two sewn in my belt. The rest has been lost to me these three days and lies with the *Sentinel*, five fathoms deep in your cove below. It is time for me to begin the world anew."

"But how about that notion o' mine?"

"We beat about the bush, I think," answered the other, pushing back his chair a bit and turning towards Ruby. "My dear young lady, your father has been begging me to stay—chiefly, no doubt, out of goodwill, but partly also that I may set him in the way to work this newly found wealth of his. I am sorry, but I must refuse."

"Why?" murmured the girl, taking courage to look at him.

"You oblige me to be brutal." His look was bent on her. He sat facing the window, and the light, as he leant sidewise, struck into the iris of his eyes and turned them blood-red in their depths. She had seen the same in dogs' eyes, but never before in a man's : and it sent a small shiver through her.

" Briefly," he went on, " I can stay on one condition only—that I marry you."

She rose from her seat and stood, grasping the back rail of the chair.

" Don't be alarmed.   I merely state the condition, but of course it's awkward : you're already bound.   Your father (who, I must say, honours me with considerable trust, seeing that he knows nothing about me) was good enough to suggest that your affection for this young fish-jowter was a transient fancy——"

" Father——" began the girl, rather for the sake of hearing her own voice than because she knew what to say.

Farmer Tresidder groaned.   " Young man, where's your gumption ?   You'm makin' a mess o't—an' I thought 'ee so very clever."

" Really," pursued the stranger imperturbably, without lifting his eyes from Ruby, " I don't know which to admire most, your father's head or his heart; his head, I think, on the whole.   So much hospitality, paternal solicitude, and commercial prudence was surely never packed into one scheme."

He broke off for a minute and, still looking at her, began to drum with his finger-tips on the cloth. His mouth was pursed up as if silently whistling an air. Ruby could neither move nor speak. The spell upon her was much like that which had lain on Young Zeb, the night before, during the hornpipe. She felt weak as a child in the presence of this man, or rather as one recovering from a long illness. He seemed to fill the room, speaking words as if they were living things, as if he were taking the world to bits and re-arranging it before her eyes. She divined the passion behind these words, and she longed to get a sight of it, to catch an echo of the voice that had sung beneath her window, an hour before. But when he resumed, it was in the same bloodless and contemptuous tone.

" Your father was very anxious that I should supplant this young jowter——"

" O Lord ! I never said it."

"Allow me," said the stranger, without deigning to look round, " to carry on this courtship in my own way. Your father, young woman, desired —it was none of my suggestion—that I should insinuate myself into your good graces. I will not conceal from you my plain opinion of your father's judgment in these matters. I think him a fool."

" Name o' thunder ! "

" Farmer, if you interrupt again I must ask you to get out. Young woman, kindly listen while I make you a formal proposition of marriage. My name, I have told you, is Zebedee Minards. I was born by London Docks, but have neither home nor people. I have travelled by land and sea ; slept on silk and straw ; drunk wine and the salt water ; fought, gambled, made love, begged my bread ; in all, lost much and found much, in many countries. I am tossed on this coast, where I find you, and find also a man in my name having hold over you. I think I want to marry you. Will you give up this other man ? "

He pursed up his lips again. With that sense of trifles which is sharpest when the world suddenly becomes too big for a human being, Ruby had a curiosity to know what he was whistling. And this worried her even

while, after a minute's silence, she stammered
out—

" I—I gave him up—last night."

" Very good. Now listen again. In an
hour's time I walk to Porthlooe. There I shall
take the van to catch the Plymouth coach. In
any case, I must spend till Saturday in Plymouth.
It depends on you whether I come back at the
end of that time. You are going to cry : keep
the tears back till you have answered me. Will
you marry me ? "

She put out a hand to steady herself, and
opened her lips. She felt the room spinning,
and wanted to cry out for mercy. But her
mouth made no sound.

" Will you marry me ? "

" Ye—e—yes ! "

As the word came, she sank down in a chair,
bent her head on the table, and burst into a
storm of tears.

" The devil's in it ! " shouted her father, and
bounced out of the room.

No sooner had the door slammed behind him
than the stranger's face became transfigured.

He stood up and laid a hand softly on the girl's head.

"Ruby!"

She did not look up. Her shoulders were shaken by one great sob after another.

"Ruby!"

He took the two hands gently from her face, and forced her to look at him. His eyes were alight with the most beautiful smile.

"For pity's sake," she cried out, "don't look at me like that. You've looked me through and through—you understand me. Don't lie with your eyes, as you're lying now."

"My dear girl, yes—I understand you. But you're wrong. I lied to get you: I'm not lying now."

"I think you must be Satan himself."

The stranger laughed. "Surely *he* needn't to have taken so much trouble. Smile back at me, Ruby, for I played a risky stroke to get you, and shall play a risky game for many days yet."

He balanced himself on the arm of her chair and drew her head towards him.

"Tell me," he said, speaking low in her ear, "if you doubt I love you. Do you know of any other man who, knowing you exactly as you are, would wish to marry you?"

She shook her head. It was impossible to lie to this man.

"Or of another who would put himself completely into your power, as I am about to do? Listen; there is no lead mine at all on Sheba farm."

Ruby drew back her face and stared at him.

"I assure you it's a fact."

"But the ore you uncovered—"

"—Was a hoax. I lied about it."

"The stuff you melted in this very fire, last might—wasn't that lead?"

"Of course it was. I stole it myself from the top of the church tower."

"Why?"

"To gain a footing here."

"Again, why?"

"For love of you."

During the silence that followed, the pair looked at each other.

H

"I am waiting for you to go and tell your father," said the stranger at length.

Ruby shivered.

"I seem to have grown very old and wise," she murmured.

He kissed her lightly.

"That's the natural result of being found out. I've felt it myself. Are you going?"

"You know that I cannot."

"You shall have twenty minutes to choose. At the end of that time I shall pass out at the gate and look up at your window. If the blind remain up, I go to the vicarage to put up our banns before I set off for Plymouth. If it be drawn down, I leave this house for ever, taking nothing from it but a suit of old clothes, a few worthless specimens (that I shall turn out of my pockets by the first hedge), and the memory of your face."

It happened, as he unlatched the gate, twenty minutes later, that the blind remained up. Ruby's face was not at the window, but he kissed his hand for all that, and smiled, and went his way singing. The air was the very same he had whistled dumbly that morning, the air that Ruby had speculated upon. And the words were—

> " ' *Soldier, soldier, will you marry me,*
>   *With the bagginet, fife and drum ?* '
> ' *Oh, no, pretty miss, I cannot marry you,*
>   *For I've got no coat to put on.* '

> " *So away she ran to the tailor's shop,*
>   *As fast as she could run,*
>   *And she bought him a coat of the very very*
>   *best,*
>   *And the soldier clapped it on.*

> " ' *Soldier, soldier, will you marry me——* ' "

His voice died away down the lane.

CHAPTER VII.

THE "JOLLY PILCHARDS."

ON the following Saturday night (New Year's Eve) an incident worth record occurred in the bar-parlour of the " Jolly Pilchards " at Porthlooe.

You may find the inn to this day on the western side of the Hauen as you go to the Old Quay. A pair of fish-scales faces the entrance, and the jolly pilchards themselves hang over your head, on a signboard that creaks mightily when the wind blows from the south.

The signboard was creaking that night, and a thick drizzle drove in gusts past the door. Behind the red blinds within, the landlady, Prudy Polwarne, stood with her back to the open hearth. Her hands rested on her hips, and the firelight, that covered all the opposite wall and most of the ceiling with her shadow, beat out between her thick ankles in the shape of a fan. She was

a widow, with a huge, pale face and a figure
nearly as broad as it was long; and no man
thwarted her.   Weaknesses she had none,
except an inability to darn her stockings.   That
the holes at her heels might not be seen, she
had a trick of pulling her stockings down under
her feet, an inch or two at a time, as they wore
out; and when the tops no longer reached to
her knee, she gartered—so gossip said—half-
way down the leg.

Around her, in as much of the warmth
as she spared, sat Old Zeb, Uncle Issy, Jim
Lewarne, his brother, and six or seven other
notables of the two parishes.   They were listening just now, and though the mug of eggy-hot
passed from hand to hand as steadily as usual,
a certain restrained excitement might have been
guessed from the volumes of smoke ascending
from their clay pipes.

"A man must feel it, boys," the hostess said,
"wi' a rale four-poster hung wi' yaller on purpose to suit his wife's complexion, an' then to
have no wife arter all."

"Ay," assented Old Zeb, who puffed in the

corner of a settle on her left, with one side of his face illuminated and the other in deep shadow, "he feels it, I b'lieve. Such a whack o' clome as he'd a-bought, and a weather-glass wherein the man comes forth as the woman goes innards, an' a dresser, painted a bright liver colour, engaging to the eye."

"I niver seed a more matterimonial outfit, as you might say," put in Uncle Issy.

"An' a warmin'-pan, an' likewise a lookin'-glass of a high pattern."

"An' what do he say?" inquired Calvin Oke, drawing a short pipe from his lips.

"In round numbers, he says nothing, but takes on."

"A wisht state!"

"Ay, 'tis wisht. Will 'ee be so good as to frisk up the beverage, Prudy, my dear?"

Prudy took up a second large mug that stood warming on the hearthstone, and began to pour the eggy-hot from one vessel to the other until a creamy froth covered the top.

"'T'other chap's a handsome chap," she said, with her eyes on her work.

"Handsome is as handsome does," squeaked Uncle Issy.

"If you wasn' such an aged man, Uncle, I'd call 'ee a very tame talker."

Uncle Issy collapsed.

"I reckon you'm all afeard o' this man," continued Prudy, looking round on the company, "else I'd have heard some mention of a shal-lal afore this."

The men with one accord drew their pipes out and looked at her.

"I mean it. If Porthlooe was the place it used to be, there'd be tin kettles in plenty to drum en out o' this naybourhood to the Rogue's March next time he showed his face here. When's he comin' back?"

No one knew.

"The girl's as bad; but 'twould be punishment enough for her to know her lover was hooted out o' the parish. Mind you, *I*'ve no grudge agen the man. I liked his dare-devil look, the only time I saw en. I'm only sayin' what I think—that you'm all afeard."

"I don't b'long to the parish," remarked a

Landaviddy man, in the pause that followed, "but 'tis incumbent on Lanihale, I'm fain to admit."

The Lanihale men fired up at this.

"I've a tin-kettle," said Calvin Oke, "an' I'm ready."

"An' I for another," said Elias Sweetland. "An' I," "An' I," echoed several voices.

"Stiddy there, stiddy, my hearts of oak," began Old Zeb, reflectively. "A still tongue makes a wise head, and 'twill be time enough to talk o' shal-lals when the weddin'-day's fixed. Now I've a better notion. It will not be gain-said by any of 'ee that I've the power of logic in a high degree—hey?"

"Trew, O king!"

"Surely, surely."

"The rarity that you be, crowder! Sorely we shall miss 'ee when you'm gone."

"Very well, then," Old Zeb announced. "I'm goin' to be logical wi' that chap. The very next time I see en, I'm goin' to step up to en an' say, as betwixt man an' man, 'Look 'ee here,' I'll say, 'I've a lawful son. You've a-took his name, an' you've a-stepped into his shoes, an' therefore I've a right to spake'" (he pulled at his churchwarden), "'to spake to 'ee'" (another pull) "'like a father.'" Here followed several pulls in quick succession.

The pipe had gone out. So, still holding the attention of the room, he reached out a hand towards the tongs. Prudy, anticipating his necessity, caught them up, dived them into the blaze, and drawing out a blazing end of stick, held it over the pipe while he sucked away.

During this pause a heavy step was heard in the passage. The door was pushed open, and a tall man, in dripping cloak and muddy boots, stalked into the room.

It was the man they had been discussing.

"A dirty night, friends, and a cold ride from Plymouth." He shook the water out of his hat over the sanded floor. "I'll take a pull at something hot, if you please."

Every one looked at him. Prudy, forgetting what she was about, waved the hot brand to and fro under Old Zeb's nose, stinging his eyes with smoke. Between confusion and suffocation, his face was a study.

"You seem astonished, all of you. May I ask why?"

"To tell 'ee the truth, young man," said Prudy, "'twas a case of 'talk of the devil an' you'll see his horns.'"

"Indeed. You were speaking good of me, I hope."

"Which o' your ears is burning?"

"Both."

"Then it shu'd be the left ear only. Old Zeb, here——"

"Hush 'ee now, Prudy!" implored the crowder.

"—Old Zeb here," continued Prudy, relentlessly, "was only a-sayin', as you walked in, that he'd read you the Riot Act afore you was many days older. He's mighty fierce wi' your goin's on, I 'sure 'ee."

"Is that so, Mr. Minards?"

Mr. Minards had, it is probable, never felt so uncomfortable in all his born days, and the experience of standing between two fires was

new to him.   He looked from the stranger
around upon the company, and was met on
all hands by the same expectant stare.

"Well, you see——" he began, and looked
around again.   The faces were inexorable.   "I
declare, friends, the pore chap is drippin' wet.
Sich a tiresome v'yage, too, as it must ha' been
from Plymouth, i' this weather !   I dunno how
we came to forget to invite en nigher the hearth.
Well, as I was a-sayin'——"

He stopped to search for his hat beneath the
settle.   Producing a large crimson handkerchief
from the crown, he mopped his brow slowly.

"The cur'ous part o't, naybours, is the
sweatiness that comes over a man, this close
weather."

"I'm waiting for your answer," put in the
stranger, knitting his brows.

"Surely, surely, that's the very thing I was
comin' to.   The answer, as you may say, is this
—but step a bit nigher, for there's lashins o'
room—the answer, as far as that goes, is what
I make to you, sayin'—that if you wasn' so
passin' wet, may be I'd blurt out what I had i'

my mind. But, as things go, 'twould seem like takin' an advantage."

"Not at all."

"'Tis very kind o' you to say so, to be sure." Old Zeb picked up his pipe again. "An' now, friends, that this little bit of onpleasantness have a-blown over, doin' ekal credit to both parties this New Year's-eve, after the native British fashion o' fair-play (as why shu'd it not?), I agree we be conformable to the pleasant season an' let harmony prevail——"

"Why, man," interrupted Prudy, "you niver gave no answer at all. 'Far as I could see you've done naught but fidget like an angletwitch and look fifty ways for Sunday."

"'Twas the roundaboutest, dodge-my-eyedest, hole-an'-cornerdest bit of a chap's mind as iver I heerd given," pronounced the traitorous Oke.

"Oke—Oke," Old Zeb exclaimed, "all you know 'pon the fiddle I taught 'ee!"

Said Prudy—"That's like what the chap said when the donkey kicked en. ' 'Taint the stummick that I do vally,' he said, ' 'tis the cussed ongratefulness o' the jackass.'"

" I'm still waiting," repeated the stranger.

" Well, then "– Old Zeb cast a rancorous look around—" I'll tell 'ee, since you'm so set 'pon hearin'. Afore you came in, the good folks here present was for drummin' you out o' the country. ' Shockin' behayviour!' 'Aw, very shockin' indeed!' was the words I heerd flyin' about, an' 'Who'll make en sensible o't?' an' 'We'll give en what-for.' 'A silent tongue makes a wise head,' said I, an' o' this I call Uncle Issy here to witness."

Uncle Issy corroborated. " You was proverbial, crowder, I can duly vow, an' to that effect, unless my mem'ry misgives me."

"So, in a mollifyin' manner, I says, ' What hev the pore chap done, to be treated so bad?' I says. Says I, ' better lave me use logic wi' en '—eh, Uncle Issy?"

" Logic was the word."

The stranger turned round upon the company, who with one accord began to look extremely foolish as Old Zeb so adroitly turned the tables.

" Is this true?" he asked.

" 'Tis the truth, I must admit," volunteered Uncle Issy, who had not been asked, but was fluttered with delight at having stuck to the right side against appearances.

"I think," said the stranger, deliberately, " it is as well that you and I, my friends, should understand each other. The turn of events has made it likely that I shall pass my days in this neighbourhood, and I wish to clear up all possible misconceptions at the start. In the first place, I am going to marry Miss Ruby Tresidder. Our banns will be asked in church to-morrow; but let us have a rehearsal. Can any man here show cause or just impediment why this marriage should not take place ? "

" You'd better ask that o' Young Zeb, mister," said Prudy.

" Why ? "

" You owe your life to'n, I hear."

" When next you see him you can put two questions. Ask him in the first place if he saved it at my request."

"Tut-tut. A man likes to live, whether he axes for it or no," grunted Elias Sweetland.

"And what the devil do you know about it?" demanded the stranger.

"I reckon I know what a man's like."

"Oh, you do, do you? Wait a while, my friend. In the second place," he went on, returning to Prudy, ask young Zebedee Minards, if he wants my life back, to come and fetch it. And now attend all. Do you see these?"

He threw back his cloak, and, diving a hand into his coat-pocket, produced a couple of pistols. The butts were rich with brass-work, and the barrels shone as he held them out in the firelight.

"You needn't dodge your heads about so gingerly. I'm only about to give you an exhibition. How many tall candlesticks have you in the house besides the pair here?" he inquired of Prudy.

"Dree pair."

"Put candles in the other two pairs and set them on the chimney-shelf."

"Why?"

"Do as I tell you."

"Now here's summat *like* a man!" said

Prudy, and went out obediently to fetch them.

Until she returned there was dead silence in the bar-parlour. The men puffed uneasily at their pipes, not one of which was alight, and avoided the stranger's eye, which rested on each in turn with a sardonic humour.

Prudy lit the candles, one from the other, and after snuffing them with her fingers that they might burn steadily, arranged them in a row on the mantelshelf. Now above this shelf the chimney-piece was panelled to the height of some two and a half feet, and along the panel certain ballads that Prudy had purchased of the Sherborne messenger were stuck in a row with pins.

"Better take those ballads down, if you value them," the stranger remarked.

She turned round inquiringly.

"I'm going to shoot."

"Sakes alive—an' my panel, an' my best brass candlesticks!"

"Take them down."

She gave in, and unpinned the ballads.

" Now stand aside."

He stepped back to the other side of the room, and set his back to the door.

" Don't move," he said to Calvin Oke, whose chair stood immediately under the line of fire, "your head is not the least in the way. And don't turn it either, but keep your eye on the candle to the right."

This was spoken in the friendliest manner, but it hardly reassured Oke, who would have preferred to keep his eye on the deadly weapon now being lifted behind his back. Nevertheless he did not disobey, but sat still, with his eyes fixed on the mantelshelf, and only his shoulders twitching to betray his discomposure.

Bang !

The room was suddenly full of sound, then of smoke and the reek of gunpowder. As the noise broke on their ears one of the candles went out quietly. The candlestick did not stir, but a bullet was embedded in the panel behind. Calvin Oke felt his scalp nervously.

" One," counted the stranger. He walked quietly to the table, set down his smoking

I

pistol, and took up the other, looking round at the same time on the white faces that stared on him behind the thick curls of smoke. Stepping back to his former position, he waited while they could count twenty, lifted the second pistol high, brought it smartly down to the aim and fired again.

The second candle went out, and a second bullet buried itself in Prudy's panel.

So he served the six, one after another, without a miss. Twice he reloaded both pistols slowly, and while he did so not a word was spoken. Indeed, the only sound to be heard came from Uncle Issy, who, being a trifle asthmatical with age, felt some inconvenience from the smoke in his throat. By the time the last shot was fired the company could hardly see one another. Prudy, two of whose dishes had been shaken off the dresser, had tumbled upon a settle, and sat there, rocking herself to and fro, with her apron over her head.

The sound of firing had reached the neigh-bouring houses, and by this time the passage

was full of men and women, agog for a tragedy.
The door burst open. Through the dense
atmosphere the stranger descried a crowd of
faces in the passage. He was the first to
speak.

"Good folk, you alarm yourselves without
cause. I have merely been pointing an argu-
ment that I and my friends happen to be
holding here."

Then he turned to Calvin Oke, who lay in
his chair like a limp sack, slowly recovering
from his emotions at hearing the bullets whiz
over his head.

"When I assure you that I carry these
weapons always about me, you will hardly
need to be warned against interfering with me
again. The first man that meddles, I'll shoot
like a rabbit—by the Lord Harry, I will! You
hear?"

He slipped the pistols into his pocket,
pulled out two crown pieces, and tossed them
to Prudy.

"That'll pay for the damage, I daresay."

So, turning on his heel, he marched out,

ɪ 2

leaving them in the firelight.   The crowd in the passage fell back to right and left, and in a moment more he had disappeared into the black drizzle outside.

But the tradition of his feat survives, and the six holes in Prudy's panel still bear witness to its truth.

CHAPTER VIII.

YOUNG ZEB SELLS HIS SOUL.

THESE things were reported to Young Zeb as he sat in his cottage, up the coombe, and nursed his pain. He was a simple youth, and took life in earnest, being very slow to catch fire, but burning consumedly when once ignited. Also he was sincere as the day, and had been treacherously used. So he raged at heart, and (for pride made him shun the public eye) he sat at home and raged—the worst possible cure for love, which goes out only by open-air treatment. From time to time his father, Uncle Issy, and Elias Sweetland sat around him and administered comfort after the manner of Eliphaz, Bildad, and Zophar.

"Your cheeks be pale, my son—lily-white, upon my soul. Rise, my son, an' eat, as the wise king recommended, sayin', 'Stay me wi' flagons, comfort me wi' yapples, for I be sick o' love.' A wise word that."

'Shall a man be poured out like water,"
inquired Uncle Issy, "an' turn from his vittles,
an' pass his prime i' blowin' his nose, an' all for
a woman ? "

"I wasn' blowin' my nose," objected Zeb,
shortly.

" Well, in black an' white you wasn', but ye
gave me that idee."

Young Zeb stared out of the window. Far
down the coombe a slice of blue sea closed the
prospect, and the tan sails of a small lugger were
visible there, rounding the point to the westward.
He watched her moodily until she passed out of
sight, and turned to his father.

" To-morrow, did 'ee say ? "

" Iss, to-morrow, at eleven i' the forenoon.
Jim Lewarne brought me word."

" Terrible times they be for Jim, I reckon,"
said Elias Sweetland. "All yestiddy he was
goin' back'ards an' forrards like a lost dog in a
fair, movin' his chattels. There's a hole in the
roof of that new cottage of his that a man may
put his Sunday hat dro'; and as for his old
woman, she'll do nought but sit 'pon the lime-

ash floor wi' her tout-serve over her head, an' call en ivery name but what he was chris'ened."

"Nothin' but neck-an'-crop would do for Tresidder, I'm told," said Old Zeb. " 'I've a-sarved 'ee faithful,' said Jim, 'an' now you turns me out wi' a week's warnin'.' "You've a-crossed my will,' says Tresidder, 'an' I've engaged a more pushin' hind in your place.' 'Tis a new fashion o' speech wi' Tresidder nowadays."

"Ay, modern words be drivin' out the old forms. But 'twas only to get Jim's cottage for that strong-will'd supplantin' furriner because Ruby said 'twas low manners for bride an' groom to go to church from the same house. So no sooner was the Lewarnes out than he was in, like shufflin' cards, wi' his marriage garment an' his brush an' comb in a hand-bag. Tresidder sent down a mattress for en, an' he slept there last night."

"Eh, but that's a trifle for a campaigner."

"Let this be a warnin' to 'ee, my son niver to save no more lives from drownin'."

"I won't," promised Young Zeb.

"We've found 'ee a great missment," Elias observed to him, after a pause. "The Psa'ms, these three Sundays, bain't what they.was for lack o' your enlivenin' flute—I can't say they be. An' to hear your very own name called forth in the banns wi' Ruby's, an' you wi'out part nor lot therein——"

"Elias, you mean it well, no doubt; but I'd take it kindly if you sheered off."

"'Twas a wisht Psa'm, too," went on Elias, "las' Sunday mornin'; an' I cudn' help my thoughts dwellin' 'pon the dismals as I blowed, nor countin' how that by this time to-morrow——"

But Young Zeb had caught up his cap and rushed from the cottage.

He took, not the highway to Porthlooe, but a footpath that slanted up the western slope of the coombe, over the brow of the hill, and led in time to the coast and a broader path above the cliffs. The air was warm, and he climbed in such hurry that the sweat soon began to drop from his forehead. By the time he reached the cliffs he was forced to pull a handkerchief out and mop himself; but without a pause, he took the turning westward towards Troy harbour, and tramped along sturdily. For his mind was made up.

Ship's-chandler Webber, of Troy, was fitting out a brand-new privateer, he had heard, and she was to sail that very week. He would go and offer himself as a seaman, and if Webber made any bones about it, he would engage to put a part of his legacy into the adventure. In fact, he was ready for anything that would take him out of Porthlooe. To live there and run the risk of meeting Ruby on the other man's arm was more than flesh and blood could stand. So he went along with his hands deep in his pockets, his eyes fastened straight ahead, his heart smoking, and the sweat stinging his eyelids. And as he went he cursed the day of his birth.

From Porthlooe to Troy Ferry is a good six miles by the cliffs, and when he had accomplished about half the distance, he was hailed by name.

Between the path at this point and the cliff's edge lay a small patch cleared for potatoes, and here an oldish man was leaning on his shovel and looking up at Zeb.

"Good-mornin', my son!"

"Mornin', hollibubber!"

The old man had once worked inland at St. Teath slate-quarries, and made his living as a "hollibubber," or one who carts away the refuse slates. On returning to his native parish he had brought back and retained the name of his profession, the parish register alone preserving his true name of Matthew Spry. He was a fervent Methodist—a local preacher, in fact—and was held in some admiration by "the people" for his lustiness in prayer-meeting. A certain intensity in his large grey eyes gave character to a face that was otherwise quite insignificant. You could see he was a good man.

"Did 'ee see that dainty frigate go cruisin' by, two hour agone?"

"No."

"Then ye missed a sweet pretty sight. Thirty guns, I do b'lieve, an' all sail set. I cou'd a'most count her guns, she stood so close."

" Hey ? "

" She tacked just here an' went round close under Bradden Point; so she's for Troy, that's certain. Be you bound that way, too ? "

" Iss, I'll see her, if she's there."

" Best not go too close, my son ; for I know the looks o' those customers. By all accounts you'm a man of too much substance to risk yourself near a press-gang."

Young Zeb gazed over the old man's head at the horizon line, and answered, as if reading the sentence there, " I might fare worse, hollibubber."

The hollibubber seemed, for a second, about to speak ; for, of course, he knew Zeb's trouble. But after a while he took his shovel out of the ground slowly.

" Ay, ye might," he said ; " pray the Lord ye don't."

Zeb went on, faster than ever. He passed Bradden Point and Widdy Cove at the rate of five miles an hour, or thereabouts ; then he turned aside over a stile and crossed a couple of meadows; and after these he was on the

high-road, on the very top of the hill over-
looking Troy Harbour.

He gazed down. The frigate was there,
as the hollibubber had guessed, anchored at
the harbour's mouth. Two men in a small
boat were pulling from her to the farther shore.
A thin haze of blue smoke lay over the town at
his feet, and the noise of mallets in the ship-
building yards came across to him through the
clear afternoon. Zeb hardly noticed all this,
for his mind was busy with a problem. He
halted by a milestone on the brow of the hill,
to consider.

And then suddenly he sat down on the stone
and shivered. The sweat was still trickling
down his face and down his back; but it had
turned cold as ice. A new idea had taken him,
an idea of which at first he felt fairly afraid.
He passed a hand over his eyes and looked down
again at the frigate. But he stared at her
stupidly, and his mind was busy with another
picture.

It occurred to him that he must go on if he
meant to arrange with Webber, that afternoon.

So he got up from the stone and went down the steep hill towards the ferry, stumbling over the rough stones in the road and hardly looking at his steps, but moving now rapidly, now slowly, like a drunken man.

The street that led down to the ferry dated back to an age before carts had superseded pack-horses, and the makers had cut it in stairs and paved it with cobbles. It plunged so steeply, and the houses on either side wedged it in so tightly, that to look down from the top was like peering into a well. A patch of blue water shone at the foot, framing a small dark square—the signboard of the " Four Lords " Inn. Just now there were two or three men gathered under the signboard.

As Young Zeb drew near he saw that they wore pig-tails and round shiny hats : and, as he noticed this, his face, which had been pale for the last five minutes, grew ashen-white. He halted for a moment, and then went on again, meaning to pass the signboard and wait on the quay for the ferry.

There were half a dozen sailors in front of

the "Four Lords." Three sat on a bench beside the door, and three more, with mugs of beer in their hands, were skylarking in the middle of the roadway.

"Hi!" called out one of those on the bench, as Zeb passed. And Zeb turned round and came to a halt again.

"What is it?"

"Where 're ye bound, mate?"

"For the ferry."

"Then stop an' drink, for the boat left two minutes since an' won't be back for another twenty."

Zeb hung on his heel for a couple of seconds. The sailor held out his mug with the friendliest air, his head thrown back and the left corner of his mouth screwed up into a smile.

"Thank 'ee," said Zeb, "I will; an' may the Lord judge 'atween us."

"There's many a way o' takin' a drink," the sailor said, staring at him; "but split me if yours ain't the rummiest *I*'ve run across."

"Oh, man, man," Zeb answered, "I wasn' thinkin' o' *you!*"

*   *   *   *   *   *

Back by the cliff's edge the hollibubber had finished his day's work and was shouldering his shovel to start for home, when he spied a dark figure coming eastwards along the track; and, putting up a hand to ward off the level rays of the sun, saw that it was the young man who had passed him at noonday. So he set down the shovel again, and waited.

Young Zeb came along with his head down. When he noticed the hollibubber standing in the path he started like a man caught in a theft.

"My son, ye 've come to lift a weight off my heart. God forgi'e me that, i' my shyness, I let 'ee go by wi'out a word for your trouble."

"All the country seems to know my affairs," Zeb answered with a scowl.

The hollibubber's grey eyes rested on him tenderly. He was desperately shy, as he had confessed: but compassion overcame his shyness.

"Surely," said he, "all we be children o' one Father: an' surely we may know each other's burdens; else, not knowin', how shall we bear 'em?"

"You'm too late, hollibubber."

Zeb stood still, looking out over the purple sea. The old man touched his arm gently.

"How so?"

"I've a-sold my soul to hell."

"I don't care. You'm alive an' standin' here, an' I can save 'ee."

"Can 'ee so?" Zeb asked ironically.

"Man, I feel sure o't." His ugly earnest face became almost grand in the flame of the sunset. "Turn aside, here, an' kneel down; I will wrestle wi' the Lord for thee till comfort comes, if it take the long night."

"You'm a strange chap. Can such things happen i' these days?"

"Kneel and try."

"No, no, no," Zeb flung out his hands. "It's too late, I tell 'ee. No man's words will I hear but the words of Lamech—'I ha' slain a man to my wounding, an' a young man to my hurt.' Let me go—'tis too late. Let me go, I say——"

As the hollibubber still clung to his arm, he gave a push and broke loose. The old man tumbled beside the path with his head against the potato fence. Zeb with a curse took to his heels and ran; nor for a hundred yards did he glance behind.

When at last he flung a look over his shoulder, the hollibubber had picked himself up and was kneeling in the pathway. His hands were clasped and lifted.

" Too late ! " shouted Zeb again, and dashed on without a second look.

J

CHAPTER IX.

YOUNG ZEB WINS HIS SOUL BACK.

At half-past nine, next morning, the stranger sat in the front room of the cottage vacated by the Lewarnes. On a rough table, pushed into a corner, lay the remains of his breakfast. A plum-coloured coat with silver buttons hung over the back of a chair by his side, and a waist-coat and silver-laced hat to match rested on the seat. For the wedding was to take place in an hour and a half.

He sat in frilled shirt, knee-breeches and stockings, and the sunlight streamed in upon his dark head as he stooped to pull on a shoe. The sound of his whistling filled the room, and the tune was, "Soldier, soldier, will you marry me?"

His foot was thrust into the first shoe, and his forefinger inserted at the heel, shoe-horn fashion, to slip it on, when the noise of light wheels sounded on the road outside, and stopped beside the gate. Looking up, he saw through the window the head and shoulders of Young Zeb's grey mare, and broke off his whistling sharply.

Rat-a-tat !

" Come in ! " he called, and smiled softly to himself.

The door was pushed open, and Young Zeb stood on the threshold, looking down on the stranger, who wheeled round quietly on his chair to face him. Zeb's clothes were disordered, and looked as if he had spent the night in them; his face was yellow and drawn, with dark semicircles underneath the eyes; and he put a hand up against the door-post for support.

" To what do I owe this honour ? " asked the stranger, gazing back at him.

Zeb pulled out a great turnip-watch from his fob, and said—

" You'm dressin'? "

" Ay, for the wedding."

" Then look sharp. You've got a bare five-an'-twenty minnits."

"Excuse me, I'm not to be married till eleven."

"Iss, iss, but *they*'re comin' at ten, sharp."

"And who in the world may 'they' be?"

"The press-gang."

The stranger sprang up to his feet, and seemed for a moment about to fly at Zeb's throat.

"You treacherous hound!"

"Stand off," said Zeb wearily, without taking his hand from the door-post. "I reckon it don't matter what I may be, or may not be, so long as you'm dressed i' ten minnits."

The other dropped his hands, with a short laugh.

"I beg your pardon. For aught I know you may have nothing to do with this infernal plot except to warn me against it."

"Don't make any mistake. 'Twas I that set the press-gang upon 'ee," answered Zeb, in the same dull tones.

There was silence between them for half a minute, and then the stranger spoke, as if to himself—

"My God! Love has made this oaf a man!" He stood for a while, sucking at his under-lip, and regarding Zeb gloomily. "May I ask why you have deliberately blown up this pretty mine at the eleventh hour?"

"I couldn't do it," Zeb groaned; "Lord knows 'twas not for love of you, but I couldn't."

"Upon my word, you fascinate me. People say that evil is more easily learnt than goodness; but that's great nonsense. The footsteps of the average beginner are equally weak in both pursuits. Would you mind telling me why you chose this particular form of treachery, in preference (let us say) to poison or shooting from behind a hedge? Was it simply because you risked less? Pardon the question, but I have a particular reason for knowing."

"We're wastin' time," said Zeb, pulling out his watch again.

"It's extraordinary how a fool will stumble on good luck. Why, sir, but for one little accident, the existence of which you could not possibly have known, I might easily have waited for the press-gang, stated the case to them, and had you lugged off to sea in my place. Has it occurred to you, in the course of your negotiations, that the wicked occasionally stumble into pits of their own digging? You, who take part in the psalm-singing every Sunday, might surely have remembered this. As it is, I suppose I must hurry on my clothes, and get to church by some roundabout way."

" I'm afeard you can't, without my help."

" Indeed ? Why ? "

" 'Cause the gang is posted all round 'ee. I met the lot half an hour back, an' promised to call 'pon you and bring word you was here."

" Come, come ; I retract my sneers. You begin to excite my admiration. I shall undoubtedly shoot you before I'm taken, but it shall be your comfort to die amid expressions of esteem."

" You'm mistaken. I came to save 'ee, if you'll be quick."

" How ? "

" I've a load of ore-weed outside, in the cart. By the lie o' the cottage none can spy ye while you slip underneath it; but I'll fetch a glance round, to make sure. Underneath it you'll be safe, and I'll drive 'ee past the sailors, and send 'em on here to search."

" You develop apace. But perhaps you'll admit a flaw in your scheme. What on earth induced you to imagine I should trust you ? "

" Man, I reckoned all that. My word's naught. But 'tis your one chance—and I would kneel to 'ee, if by kneelin' I could persuade 'ee. We'll fight it out after; bring your pistols. Only come ! "

The stranger slipped on his other shoe, then his waistcoat and jacket, whistling softly. Then he stepped to the chimney-piece, took down his pistols, and stowed them in his coat-pockets.

" I'm quite ready."

Zeb heaved a great sigh like a sob; but only said :—

" Wait a second while I see that the coast's clear."

In less than three minutes the stranger was packed under the evil-smelling weed, drawing breath with difficulty, and listening, when the jolting allowed, to Zeb's voice as he encouraged the mare. Jowters' carts travel fast as a rule, for their load perishes soon, and the distance from the coast to the market is often considerable. In this case Jessamy went at a round gallop, the loose stones flying from under her hoofs. Now and then one struck up against the bottom of the cart. It was hardly pleasant to be rattled at this rate, Heaven knew whither. But the stranger had chosen his course, and was not the man to change his mind.

After about five minutes of this the cart was pulled up with a scramble, and he heard a voice call out, as it seemed, from the hedge—

"Well?"

"Right you are," answered Young Zeb; "He's in the front room, pullin' on his boots. You'd best look slippy."

"Where's the coin?"

"There!" The stranger heard the click of money, as of a purse being caught. "You'll find it all right."

"H'm; best let me count it, though. One—

two—three—four. I feels it my dooty to tell ye, young man, that it be a dirty trick. If this didn't chime in wi' my goodwill towards his Majesty's service, be danged if I'd touch the job with a pair o' tongs!"

"Ay—but I reckon you'll do't, all the same, for t'other half that's to come when you've got en safe an' sound. Dirty hands make clean money."

"Well, well; ye've been dirtily sarved. I'll see 'ee this arternoon at the 'Four Lords.' We've orders to sail at five, sharp; so there's no time to waste."

"Then I won't detain 'ee. Clk, Jessamy!"

The jolting began again, more furiously than ever, as the stranger drew a long breath. He waited till he judged they must be out of sight, and then began to stir beneath his load of weed.

"Keep quiet," said Zeb; "you shall get out as soon as we're up the hill."

The cart began to move more slowly, and tilted back with a slant that sent the stranger's heels against the tail-board. Zeb jumped down and trudged at the side. The hill was long, and steep from foot to brow; and when at length the slope lessened, the wheels turned off at a sharp angle and began to roll softly over turf.

The weight and smell of the weed were beginning to suffocate the man beneath it, when Zeb called out "Woa-a!" and the mare stopped.

" Now you can come out."

The other rose on his knees, shook some of his burden off, and blinked in the strong sunlight.

The cart stood on the fringe of a desolate tract of downs, high above the coast. Over the hedge to the right appeared a long narrow strip of sea. On the three remaining sides nothing was visible but undulating stretches of brown turf, except where, to northward, the summits of two hills in the heart of the county just topped the rising ground that hid twenty intervening miles of broken plain.

" We can leave the mare to crop. There's a hollow, not thirty yards off, that'll do for us."

Zeb led the way to the spot. It was indeed the fosse of a half-obliterated Roman camp, and ran at varying depth around a cluster of grassy mounds, the most salient of which—the præ-torian—still served as a landmark for the Porthlooe fishing boats. But down in the fosse the pair were secure from all eyes. Not a word was spoken until they stood together at the bottom.

Here Zeb pulled out his watch once more.

"We'd best be sharp," he said; "you must start in twenty minnits to get to the church in time."

"It would be interesting to know what you propose doing." The stranger sat down on the slope, picked a strip of sea-weed off his breeches, and looked up with a smile.

"I reckon you'll think it odd."

"Of that I haven't a doubt."

"Well, you've a pair o' pistols i' your pockets, an' they're loaded, I expect."

"They are."

"I'd a notion of askin' 'ee, as a favour, to give and take a shot with me."

The stranger paused a minute before giving his answer.

" Can you fire a pistol ? "

" I've let off a blunderbust, afore now, an' I suppose 'tis the same trick."

" And has it struck you that your body may be hard to dispose of?   Or that, if found, it may cause me some inconvenience ? "

" There's a quag on t'other side o' the Castle * here.   I han't time to go round an' point it out; but 'tis to be known by bein' greener than the rest o' the turf.   What's thrown in there niver comes up, an' no man can dig for it.   The folks 'll give the press-gang the credit when I'm missin'——"

" You forget the mare and cart."

" Lead her back to the road, turn her face to home, an' fetch her a cut across th' ears.   She always bolts if you touch her ears."

" And you really wish to die ? "

" Oh, my God ! " Zeb broke out ; " would I be standin' here if I didn' ? "

* Camp.

The stranger rose to his feet, and drew out his pistols slowly.

" It's a thousand pities," he said ; " for I never saw a man develop character so fast."

He cocked the triggers, and handed the pistols to Zeb, to take his choice.

" Stand where you are, while I step out fifteen paces." He walked slowly along the fosse, and, at the end of that distance, faced about. " Shall I give the word ? "

Zeb nodded, watching him sullenly.

" Very well. I shall count three slowly, and after that we can fire as we please. Are you ready?—stand a bit sideways. Your chest is a pretty broad target—that's right; I'm going to count. *One—two—three—*"

The word was hardly spoken before one of the pistols rang out. It was Zeb's; and Heaven knows whither his bullet flew. The smoke cleared away in a blue, filmy streak, and revealed his enemy standing where he stood before, with his pistol up, and a quiet smile on his face.

Still holding the pistol up, the stranger

now advanced deliberately until he came to a
halt about two paces from Zeb, who, with white
face and set jaw, waited for the end. The eyes
of the two men met, and neither flinched.

"Strip," commanded the stranger. "Strip
—take off that jersey."

"Why not kill me without ado? Man, isn't
this cruel?"

"Strip, I say."

Zeb stared at him for half a minute, like
a man in a trance; and began to pull the
jersey off.

"Now your shirt. Strip—till you are
naked as a babe."

Zeb obeyed. The other laid his pistol down
on the turf, and also proceeded to undress, until
the two men stood face to face, stark naked.

"We were thus, or nearly thus, a month
ago, when you gave me my life. Does it strike
you that, barring our faces, we might be twin
brothers? Now, get into my clothes, and toss
me over your own!"

"What's the meanin' o't?" stammered Zeb,
hoarsely.

"I am about to cry quits with you. Hurry; for the bride must be at the church by this."

"What's the meanin' o't?" Zeb repeated.

"Why, that you shall marry the girl. Steady—don't tremble. The banns are up in your name, and you shall walk into church, and the woman shall be married to Zebedee Minards. Stop, don't say a word, or I'll repent and blow your brains out. You want to know who I am, and what's to become of me. Suppose I'm the Devil; suppose I'm your twin soul, and in exchange for my life have given you the half of manhood that you lacked and I possessed; suppose I'm just a deserter from his Majesty's fleet, a poor devil of a marine, with gifts above his station, who ran away and took to privateering, and was wrecked at your doors. Suppose that I am really Zebedee Minards; or suppose that I heard your name spoken in Sheba kitchen, and took a fancy to wear it myself. Suppose that I shall vanish to-day in a smell of brimstone; or that I shall leave in irons in the hold of the frigate now in Troy harbour. What's her name?"

He was dressed by this time in Zeb's old clothes.

" The *Recruit.*"

" Whither bound ? "

" Back to Plymouth to-night, an' then to the West Indies wi' a convoy."

" Hurry, then ; don't fumble, or Ruby 'll be tired of waiting.   You'll find a pencil and scrap of paper in my breast pocket.   Hand them over."

Zeb did so, and the stranger, seating himself again on the slope, tore the paper in half, and began to scribble a few lines on each piece.   By the time he had finished and folded them up, Zeb stood before him dressed in the plum-coloured suit.

" Ay," said the stranger, looking him up and down, and sucking the pencil contempla-tively ; " she'll marry you out of hand."

" I doubt it."

" These notes will make sure.   Give one to the farmer, and one to Ruby, as they stand by the chancel rails.   But mainly it rests with you. Take no denial.   Say you've come to make her your wife, and won't leave the church till you've done it. She's still the same woman as when she threw you over. Ah, sir, we men change our natures; but woman is always Eve. I suppose you know a short cut to the church? Very well. I shall take your cart and mare, and drive to meet the press-gang, who won't be in the sweetest of tempers just now. Come, what are you waiting for? You're ten minutes late as it is, and you can't be married after noon."

"Sir," said Zeb, with a white face; "it's a liberty, but will 'ee let me shake your hand?"

"I'll be cursed if I do. But I'll wish you good luck and a hard heart, and maybe ye'll thank me some day."

So Zeb, with a sob, turned and ran from him out of the fosse and towards a gap in the hedge, where lay a short cut through the fields. In the gap he turned and looked back. The stranger stood on the lip of the fosse, and waved a hand to him to hurry.

K

CHAPTER X.

THE THIRD SHIP.

WE return to Ruan church, whence this history started. The parson was there in his surplice, by the altar; the bride was there in her white frock, by the chancel rails; her father, by her side, was looking at his watch; and the parishioners thronged the nave, shuffling their feet and loudly speculating. For the bridegroom had not appeared.

Ruby's face was white as her frock. Parson Babbage kept picking up the heavy Prayerbook, opening it, and laying it down impatiently. Occasionally, as one of the congregation scraped an impatient foot, a metallic sound made itself heard, and the buzz of conversation would sink for a moment, as if by magic.

For beneath the seats, and behind the women's gowns, the whole pavement of the church was covered with a fairly representative collection of cast-off kitchen utensils—old kettles, broken cake-tins, frying-pans, saucepans—all calculated to emit dismal sounds under percussion. Scattered among these were ox-bells, rook-rattles, a fog-horn or two, and a tin trumpet from Liskeard fair. Explanation is simple : the outraged feelings of the parish were to be avenged by a shal-lal as bride and bridegroom left the church. Ruby knew nothing of the storm brewing for her, but Mary Jane, whose ears had been twice boxed that morning, had heard a whisper of it on her way down to the church, and was confirmed in her fears by observing the few members of the congregation who entered after her. Men and women alike suffered from an unwonted corpulence and tightness of raiment that morning, and each and all seemed to have cast the affliction off as they arose from their knees. It was too late to interfere, so she sat still and trembled.

Still the bridegroom did not come.

" A more onpresidented feat I don't recall," remarked Uncle Issy to a group that stood at the west end under the gallery, " not since 'Melia Spry's buryin', when the devil, i' the

shape of a black pig, followed us all the way
to the porch."

" That was a brave while ago, Uncle."

"Iss, iss; but I mind to this hour how we
bearers perspired—an' she such a light-weight
corpse.   But plague seize my old emotions !—
we'm come to marry, not to bury."

" By the look o't 'tis neither marry nor
bury, Nim nor Doll," observed Old Zeb, who
had sacrificed his paternal feelings and come to
church in order to keep abreast with the age;
" 'tis more like Boscastle Fair, begin at twelve
o'clock an' end at noon.   Why tarry the wheels
of his chariot ? "

" 'Tis possible Young Zeb an' he have a-met
'pon the road hither," hazarded Calvin Oke by a
wonderful imaginative effort ; " an' 'tis possible
that feelings have broke loose an' one o' the
twain be swelterin' in his own bloodshed, or
vicey-versey."

" I heard tell of a man once," said Uncle
Issy, " that committed murder upon another for
love ; but, save my life, I can't think 'pon his
name, nor where 't befell."

" What an old store-house 'tis ! " ejaculated Elias Sweetland, bending a contemplative gaze on Uncle Issy.

" Mark her pale face, naybours," put in a woman ; " an' Tresidder, he looks like a man that's neither got nor lost."

" Trew, trew."

" Quarter past the hour, I make it," said Old Zeb, pulling out his timepiece.

Still the bridegroom tarried.

Higher up the church, in the front pew but one, Modesty Prowse said aloud to Sarah Ann Nanjulian—

" If he doesn' look sharp, we'll be married before she after all."

Ruby heard the sneer, and answered it with a look of concentrated spite. Probably she would have risked her dignity to retort, had not Parson Babbage advanced down the chancel at this juncture.

" Has anyone seen the bridegroom to-day ? " he inquired of Tresidder. " Or will you send some one to hurry him ? "

" Be danged if I know," the farmer began

testily, mopping his bald head, and then he broke off, catching sound of a stir among the folk behind.

" Here he be—here he be at last!" cried somebody. And with that a hush of bewilderment fell on the congregation.

In the doorway, flushed with running and glorious in bridal attire, stood Young Zeb.

It took everybody's breath away, and he walked up the nave between silent men and women. His eyes were fastened on Ruby, and she in turn stared at him as a rabbit at a snake, shrinking slightly on her father's arm. Tresidder's jaw dropped, and his eyes began to protrude.

" What's the meanin' o' this?" he stammered.

" I've come to marry your daughter," answered Zeb, very slow and distinct. " She was to wed Zebedee Minards to-day, an' I'm Zebedee Minards."

" But——"

" I've a note to hand to each of 'ee. Better save your breath till you've read 'em."

He delivered the two notes, and stood, tapping a toe on the tiles, in the bridegroom's place on the right of the chancel-rails.

"Damnation!"

"Mr. Tresidder," interrupted the parson, "I like a man to swear off his rage if he's upset, but I can't allow it in the church."

"I don't care if you do or you don't."

"Then do it, and I'll kick you out with this very boot."

The farmer's face was purple, and big veins stood out by his temples.

"I've been cheated," he growled.

Zeb, who had kept his eyes on Ruby, stepped quickly towards her. First picking up the paper that had drifted to the pavement, he crushed it into his pocket. He then took her hand. It was cold and damp.

"Parson, will 'ee marry us up, please?"

"You haven't asked if she'll have you."

"No, an' I don't mean to. I didn't come to ax questions—that's your business—but to answer."

"Will you marry this man?" demanded the parson, turning to Ruby.

Zeb's hand still enclosed hers, and she felt she was caught and held for life. Her eyes fluttered up to her lover's face, and found it inexorable.

" Yes," she gasped out, as if the word had been suffocating her. And with the word came a rush of tears—helpless, but not altogether unhappy.

" Dry your eyes," said Parson Babbage, after waiting a minute; " we must be quick about it."

So it happened that the threatened shal-lal came to nothing. Susan Jago, the old woman who swept the church, discovered its forgotten apparatus scattered beneath the pews on the following Saturday, and cleared it out, to the amount (she averred) of two cartloads. She tossed it, bit by bit, over the west wall of the churchyard, where in time it became a mound, covered high with sting-nettles. If you poke among these nettles with your walking-stick, the odds are that you turn up a scrap of rusty iron. But there exists more explicit testimony to Zeb's wedding within the church—and within the churchyard, too, where he and Ruby have rested this many a year.

Though the bubble of Farmer Tresidder's dreams was pricked that day, there was feasting at Sheba until late in the evening. Nor until eleven did the bride and bridegroom start off, arm in arm, to walk to their new home. Before them, at a considerable distance, went the players and singers—a black blur on the moonlit road; and very crisply their music rang out beneath a sky scattered with cloud and stars. All their songs were simple carols of the country, and the burden of them was but the joy of man at Christ's nativity; but the young man and maid who walked behind were well pleased.

"Now then," cried the voice of Old Zeb, "lads an' lasses all together an' wi' a will——

> " *All under the leaves, an' the leaves o' life,*
> *I met wi' virgins seven,*
> *An' one o' them was Mary mild,*
> *Our Lord's mother of Heaven.*

' *O what are 'ee seekin', you seven fair maids,*
  All under the leaves o' life ;
Come tell, come tell, what seek ye
  All under the leaves o' life ? '

' *We're seekin' for no leaves, Thomas,*
  But for a friend o' thine,
We're seekin' for sweet Jesus Christ
  To be our guide an' thine.'

' *Go down, go down, to yonder town*
  An' sit in the gallery,
An' there you'll see sweet Jesus Christ
  Nailed to a big yew-tree.'

So down they went to yonder town
  As fast as foot could fall,
An' many a grievous bitter tear
  From the Virgin's eye did fall.

' *O peace, Mother—O peace, Mother,*
  Your weepin' doth me grieve ;
I must suffer this,' he said,
  ' *For Adam an' for Eve.*

‘ *O Mother, take John Evangelist*
    All for to be your son,
An' he will comfort you sometimes
    Mother, as I've a-done.'

‘ *O come, thou John Evangelist,*
    Thou'rt welcome unto me,
But more welcome my own dear Son
    Whom I nursed on my knee.'

Then he laid his head 'pon his right shoulder
    Seein' death it struck him nigh ;
‘ *The holy Mother be with your soul—*
    I die, Mother, I die.'

O the rose, the gentle rose,
    An' the fennel that grows so green !
God gi'e us grace in every place
    To pray for our king an' queen.

Furthermore, for our enemies all
    Our prayers they should be strong ;
Amen, good Lord ; your charity
    Is the endin' of my song ! ”

In the midst of this carol Ruby, with a light pull on Zeb's arm, brought him to a halt.

"How lovely it all is, Zeb!" She looked upwards at the flying moon, then dropped her gaze over the frosty sea, and sighed gently. "Just now I feel as if I'd been tossin' out yonder through many fierce days an' nights an' were bein' taken at last to a safe haven. You'll have to make a good wife of me, Zeb. I wonder if you'll do 't."

Zeb followed the direction of her eyes, and seemed to discern off Bradden Point a dot of white, as of a ship in sail. He pressed her arm to his side, but. said nothing.

"Clear your throats, friends," shouted his father, up the road, " an' let fly—

"*As I sat on a sunny bank,*
　　　—A sunny bank, a sunny bank,
As I sat on a sunny bank
On Chris'mas day i' the mornin',

I saw dree ships come sailin' by,
  —A-sailin' by, a-sailin' by,
I saw dree ships come sailin' by
On Chris'mas day i' the mornin'.

Now who shud be i' these dree ships——"

And to this measure Zeb and Ruby stepped home.

At the cottage door Zeb thanked the singers, who went their way and flung back shouts and joyful wishes as they went. Before making all fast for the night, he stood a minute or so, listening to their voices as they died away down the road. As he barred the door, he turned and saw that Ruby had lit the lamp, and was already engaged in setting the kitchen to rights; for, of course, no such home-coming had been dreamt of in the morning, and all was in disorder. He stood and watched her for a while, then turned to the window.

After a minute or two, finding that he did not speak, she too came to the window. He bent and kissed her.

For he had seen, on the patch of sea beyond the haven, a white frigate steal up Channel like a ghost. She had passed out of his sight by this time, but he was still thinking of one man that she bore.

THE HAUNTED DRAGOON.

THE
HAUNTED DRAGOON.

Beside the Plymouth road, as it plunges down-
hill past Ruan Lanihale church towards Ruan
Cove, and ten paces beyond the lych-gate—
where the graves lie level with the coping, and
the horseman can decipher their inscriptions in
passing, at the risk of a twisted neck—the base
of the churchyard wall is pierced with a low
archway, festooned with toad-flax and fringed
with the hart's-tongue fern. Within the archway bubbles a well, the water of which was once
used for all baptisms in the parish, for no child
sprinkled with it could ever be hanged with
hemp. But this belief is discredited now, and
the well neglected: and the events which led to
this are still a winter's tale in the neighbourhood. I set them down as they were told me,

L

across the blue glow of a wreck-wood fire, by
Sam Tregear, the parish bedman. Sam himself
had borne an inconspicuous share in them; and
because of them Sam's father had carried a
white face to his grave.

My father and mother (said Sam) married
late in life, for his trade was what mine is, and
'twasn't till her fortieth year that my mother
could bring herself to kiss a gravedigger. That
accounts, maybe, for my being born rickety and
with other drawbacks that only made father the
fonder. Weather permitting, he'd carry me off
to churchyard, set me upon a flat stone, with his
coat folded under, and talk to me while he
delved. I can mind, now, the way he'd settle
lower and lower, till his head played hidey-peep
with me over the grave's edge, and at last he'd
be clean swallowed up, but still discoursing or
calling up how he'd come upon wonderful towns
and kingdoms down underground, and how all
the kings and queens there, in dyed garments,
was offering him meat for his dinner every day
of the week if he'd only stop and hobbynob

with them—and all such gammut. He prettily
doted on me—the poor old ancient !

But there came a day—a dry afternoon in
the late wheat harvest—when we were up in the
churchyard together, and though father had his
tools beside him, not a tint did he work, but kept
travishing back and forth, one time shading his
eyes and gazing out to sea, and then looking
far along the Plymouth road for minutes at a
time. Out by Bradden Point there stood a
little dandy-rigged craft, tacking lazily to and
fro, with her mains'le all shiny-yellow in the
sunset. Though I didn't know it then, she was
the Preventive boat, and her business was to
watch the Hauen : for there had been a brush
between her and the *Unity* lugger, a fortnight
back, and a Preventive man shot through the
breast-bone and my mother's brother Philip
was hiding down in the town. I minded, later,
how that the men across the vale, in Farmer
Tresidder's wheat-field, paused every now and
then, as they pitched the sheaves, to give a look
up towards the churchyard, and the gleaners
moved about in small knots, causeying and

L 2

glancing over their shoulders at the cutter out
in the bay; and how, when all the field was
carried, they waited round the last load, no man
offering to cry the *Neck*, as the fashion was, but
lingering till sun was near down behind the
slope and the long shadows stretching across
the stubble.

"Sha'n't thee go underground to-day,
father?" says I, at last.

He turned slowly round, and says he, "No,
sonny. 'Reckon us 'll climb skywards for a
change."

And with that, he took my hand, and
pushing abroad the belfry door began to climb
the stairway. Up and up, round and round we
went, in a sort of blind-man's-holiday full of
little glints of light and whiffs of wind where
the open windows came; and at last stepped
out upon the leads of the tower and drew
breath.

"There's two-an'-twenty parishes to be witnessed from where we're standin', sonny—if
ye've got eyes," says my father.

Well, first I looked down towards the

harvesters and laughed to see them so small: and then I fell to counting the church-towers dotted across the high-lands, and seeing if I could make out two-and-twenty. 'Twas the prettiest sight—all the country round looking as if 'twas dusted with gold, and the Plymouth road winding away over the hills like a long white tape. I had counted thirteen churches, when my father pointed his hand out along this road and called to me—

" Look'ee out yonder, honey, an' say what ye see ! "

" I see dust," says I.

" Nothin' else ? Sonny boy, use your eyes, for mine be dim."

" I see dust," says I again, " an' suthin' twinklin' in it, like a tin can——"

" Dragooners ! " shouts my father ; and then, running to the side of the tower facing the harvest-field, he put both hands to his mouth and called :

" *What have 'ee ? What have 'ee ?* "

— very loud and long.

"*A neck—a neck !* " came back from the

field, like as if all shouted at once—dear, the
sweet sound! And then a gun was fired, and
craning forward over the coping I saw a dozen
men running across the stubble and out into the
road towards the Hauen; and they called as
they ran, "*A neck—a neck!*"

"Iss," says my father, "'tis a neck, sure
'nuff. Pray God they save en! Come,
sonny——"

But we dallied up there till the horsemen
were plain to see, and their scarlet coats and
armour blazing in the dust as they came. And
when they drew near within a mile, and our
limbs ached with crouching — for fear they
should spy us against the sky—father took me
by the hand and pulled hot foot down the
stairs. Before they rode by he had picked up
his shovel and was shovelling out a grave for
his life.

Forty valiant horsemen they were, riding
two-and-two (by reason of the narrowness of the
road) and a captain beside them—men broad and
long, with hairy top-lips, and all clad in scarlet
jackets and white breeches that showed bravely

against their black war-horses and jet-black
holsters, thick as they were wi' dust. Each man
had a golden helmet, and a scabbard flapping by
his side, and a piece of metal like a half-moon
jingling from his horse's cheek-strap. 12 D was
the numbering on every saddle, meaning the
Twelfth Dragoons.

Tramp, tramp! they rode by, talking and
joking, and taking no more heed of me—that sat
upon the wall with my heels dangling above them
—than if I'd been a sprig of stonecrop. But the
captain, who carried a drawn sword and mopped
his face with a handkerchief so that the dust ran
across it in streaks, drew rein, and looked over
my shoulder to where father was digging.

"Sergeant!" he calls back, turning with a
hand upon his crupper; "didn't we see a figger
like this a-top o' the tower, some way back?"

The sergeant pricked his horse forward and
saluted. He was the tallest, straightest man in
the troop, and the muscles on his arm filled out
his sleeve with the three stripes upon it—a
handsome red-faced fellow, with curly black
hair.

Says he, "That we did, sir—a man with sloping shoulders and a boy with a goose neck." Saying this, he looked up at me with a grin.

"I'll bear it in mind," answered the officer, and the troop rode on in a cloud of dust, the sergeant looking back and smiling, as if 'twas a joke that he shared with us. Well, to be short, they rode down into the town as night fell. But 'twas too late, Uncle Philip having had fair warning and plenty of time to flee up towards the little secret hold under Mabel Down, where none but two families knew how to find him. All the town, though, knew he was safe, and lashins of women and children turned out to see the comely soldiers hunt in vain till ten o'clock at night.

The next thing was to billet the warriors. The captain of the troop, by this, was pesky cross-tempered, and flounced off to the "Jolly Pilchards" in a huff. "Sergeant," says he, "here's an inn, though a damned bad 'un, an' here I means to stop. Somewheres about there's a farm called Constantine, where I'm told the men can be accommodated. Find out the place, if you can, an' do your best: an' don't let me see yer face till to-morra," says he.

So Sergeant Basket—that was his name— gave the salute, and rode his troop up the street, where—for his manners were mighty winning, notwithstanding the dirty nature of his errand— he soon found plenty to direct him to Farmer Noy's, of Constantine; and up the coombe they rode into the darkness, a dozen or more going along with them to show the way, being won by their martial bearing as well as the sergeant's very friendly way of speech.

Farmer Noy was in bed—a pock-marked, lantern-jawed old gaffer of sixty-five; and the most remarkable point about him was the wife he had married two years before—a young slip of a girl but just husband-high. Money did it, I reckon; but if so, 'twas a bad bargain for her. He was noted for stinginess to such a degree that they said his wife wore a brass wedding-ring, weekdays, to save the genuine article from wear- ing out. She was a Ruan woman, too, and therefore ought to have known all about him. But woman's ways be past finding out.

Hearing the hoofs in his yard and the sergeant's *stram-a-ram* upon the door, down comes the old curmudgeon with a candle held high above his head.

" What the devil's here?" he calls out.

Sergeant Basket looks over the old man's shoulder; and there, halfway up the stairs, stood Madam Noy in her night rail—a high-coloured ripe girl, languishing for love, her red lips parted and neck all lily-white against a loosened pile of dark-brown hair.

" Be cussed if I turn back ! " said the sergeant to himself ; and added out loud—

" Forty souldjers, in the King's name ! "

" Forty devils ! " says old Noy.

" They're devils to eat," answered the sergeant, in the most friendly manner ; " an', begad, ye must feed an' bed 'em this night— or else I'll search your cellars.   Ye are a loyal man —eh, farmer?   An' your cellars are big, I'm told."

" Sarah," calls out the old man, following the sergeant's bold glance, " go back an' dress yersel' dacently this instant !   These here honest

souldjers—forty damned honest gormandisin'
souldjers—be come in his Majesty's name, forty
strong, to protect honest folks' rights in the
intervals of eatin' 'em out o' house an' home.
Sergeant, ye be very welcome i' the King's name.
Cheese an' cider ye shall have, an' I pray the
mixture may turn your forty stomachs."

In a dozen minutes he had fetched out his
stable-boys and farm-hands, and, lantern in hand,
was helping the sergeant to picket the horses
and stow the men about on clean straw in the
outhouses.   They were turning back to the
house, and the old man was turning over in his
mind that the sergeant hadn't yet said a word
about where he was to sleep, when by the door
they found Madam Noy waiting, in her
wedding gown, and with her hair freshly
braided.

Now, the farmer was mortally afraid of the
sergeant, knowing he had thirty ankers and more
of contraband liquor in his cellars, and minding
the sergeant's threat.   None the less his jealousy
got the upper hand.

" Woman," he cries out, " to thy bed !"

" I was waiting," said she, " to say the Cap'n's bed——"

" Sergeant's," says the dragoon, correcting her.

"—Was laid i' the spare room."

" Madam," replies Sergeant Basket, looking into her eyes and bowing, " a soldier with my responsibility sleeps but little. In the first place, I must see that my men sup."

" The maids be now cuttin' the bread an' cheese and drawin' the cider."

" Then, Madam, leave me but possession of the parlour, and let me have a chair to sleep in."

By this they were in the passage together, and her gaze devouring his regimentals. The old man stood a pace off, looking sourly. The sergeant fed his eyes upon her, and Satan got hold of him.

" Now if only," said he, " one of you could play cards ! "

" But I must go to bed," she answered ; " though I can play cribbage, if only you stay another night."

For she saw the glint in the farmer's eye ;

and so Sergeant Basket slept bolt upright that night in an arm-chair by the parlour fender. Next day the dragooners searched the town again, and were billeted all about among the cottages. But the sergeant returned to Constantine, and before going to bed—this time in the spare room—played a game of cribbage with Madam Noy, the farmer smoking sulkily in his arm-chair.

"Two for his heels!" said the rosy woman suddenly, halfway through the game. "Sergeant, you're cheatin' yoursel' an' forgettin' to mark. Gi'e me the board; I'll mark for both."

She put out her hand upon the board, and Sergeant Basket's closed upon it. 'Tis true he had forgot to mark; and feeling the hot pulse in her wrist, and beholding the hunger in her eyes, 'tis to be supposed he'd have forgot his own soul.

He rode away next day with his troop: but my uncle Philip not being caught yet, and the Government set on making an example of him, we hadn't seen the last of these dragoons. 'Twas a time of fear down in the town. At dead of night or at noonday they came on us—six times

in all: and for two months the crew of the
Unity couldn't call their souls their own, but
lived from day to day in secret closets and
wandered the country by night, hiding in
hedges and straw-houses. All that time the
revenue men watched the Hauen, night and day,
like dogs before a rat-hole.

But one November morning 'twas whispered
abroad that Uncle Philip had made his way to
Falmouth, and slipped across to Guernsey. Time
passed on, and the dragooners were seen no more,
nor the handsome devil-may-care face of Sergeant Basket. Up at Constantine, where he had
always contrived to billet himself, 'tis to be
thought pretty Madam Noy pined to see him
again, kicking his spurs in the porch and smiling
out of his gay brown eyes; for her face fell away
from its plump condition, and the hunger in her
eyes grew and grew. But a more remarkable
fact was that her old husband—who wouldn't
have yearned after the dragoon, ye'd have
thought—began to dwindle and fall away too.
By the New Year he was a dying man, and
carried his doom on his face. And on New

Year's Day he straddled his mare for the last time, and rode over to Looe, to Doctor Gale's.

"Goody - losh!" cried the doctor, taken aback by his appearance—"What's come to ye, Noy?"

"Death!" says Noy. "Doctor, I bain't come for advice, for before this day week I'll be a clay-cold corpse. I come to ax a favour. When they summon ye, before lookin' at my body—that 'll be past help—go you to the little left-top corner drawer o' my wife's bureau, an' there ye 'll find a packet. You 're my executor," says he, "and I leaves ye to deal wi' that packet as ye thinks fit."

With that, the farmer rode away home-along, and the very day week he went dead.

The doctor, when called over, minded what the old chap had said, and sending Madam Noy on some pretence to the kitchen, went over and unlocked the little drawer with a duplicate key, that the farmer had unhitched from his watch-chain and given him. There was no parcel of letters, as he looked to find, but only a small packet crumpled away in the corner. He pulled it out and gave a look, and a sniff, and another look : then shut the drawer, locked it, strode straight down-stairs to his horse and galloped away.

In three hours' time, pretty Madam Noy was in the constables' hands upon the charge of murdering her husband by poison.

They tried her, next Spring Assize, at Bodmin, before the Lord Chief Justice. There wasn't evidence enough to put Sergeant Basket in the dock alongside of her—though 'twas freely guessed he knew more than anyone (saving the prisoner herself) about the arsenic that was found in the little drawer and inside the old man's body. He was subpœna'd from Plymouth, and cross-examined by a great hulking King's Counsel for three-quarters of an hour. But they got nothing out of him. All through the examination the prisoner looked at him and nodded her white face, every now and then, at his answers, as much as to say, " That's right—that's right : they shan't harm thee, my dear." And the love-light shone in her eyes for all the court to see. But the sergeant never let his look meet it. When he stepped down at last she gave a sob of joy, and fainted bang-off.

They roused her up, after this, to hear the verdict of *Guilty* and her doom spoken by the judge. "Pris'ner at the bar," said the Clerk of Arraigns, "have ye anything to say why this court should not pass sentence o' death?"

She held tight of the rail before her, and spoke out loud and clear—

"My Lord and gentlemen all, I be a guilty woman; an' I be ready to die at once for my sin. But if ye kill me now, ye kill the child in my body—an' he is innocent."

Well, 'twas found she spoke truth; and the hanging was put off till after the time of her delivery. She was led back to prison, and there, about the end of June, her child was born, and died before he was six hours old. But the mother recovered, and quietly abode the time of her hanging.

I can mind her execution very well; for

M

father and mother had determined it would be an excellent thing for my rickets to take me into Bodmin that day, and get a touch of the dead woman's hand, which in those times was considered an unfailing remedy. So we borrowed the parson's manure-cart, and cleaned it thoroughly, and drove in together.

The place of the hangings, then, was a little door in the prison-wall, looking over the bank where the railway now goes, and a dismal piece of water called Jail-pool, where the townsfolk drowned most of the dogs and cats they'd no further use for. All the bank under the gallows was that thick with people you could almost walk upon their heads; and my ribs were squeezed by the crowd so that I couldn't breathe freely for a month after. Back across the pool, the fields along the side of the valley were lined with booths and sweet-stalls and standings—a perfect Whitsun-fair; and a din going up that cracked your ears.

But there was the stillness of death when the woman came forth, with the sheriff and the chaplain reading in his book, and the unnamed

man behind—all from the little door. She wore
a strait black gown, and a white kerchief about
her neck—a lovely woman, young and white and
tearless.

She ran her eye over the crowd and stepped
forward a pace, as if to speak; but lifted a finger
and beckoned instead : and out of the people a
man fought his way to the foot of the scaffold.
'Twas the dashing sergeant, that was here upon
sick-leave. Sick he was, I believe. His face
above his shining regimentals was grey as a
slate; for he had committed perjury to save his
skin, and on the face of the perjured no sun will
ever shine.

" Have you got it ? " the doomed woman said,
many hearing the words.

He tried to reach, but the scaffold was too
high, so he tossed up what was in his hand, and
the woman caught it—a little screw of tissue-
paper.

"I must see that, please ! " said the sheriff,
laying a hand upon her arm.

" 'Tis but a weddin'-ring, sir "—and she
slipped it over her finger. Then she kissed it
M 2

once, under the beam, and, lookin' into the
dragoon's eyes, spoke very slow—

"*Husband, our child shall go wi' you; an'
when I want you he shall fetch you.*"

—and with that turned to the sheriff, saying :
" I be ready, sir."

The sheriff wouldn't give father and mother
leave for me to touch the dead woman's hand ; so
they drove back that evening grumbling a good
bit.   'Tis a sixteen-mile drive, and the ostler in
at Bodmin had swindled the poor old horse out
of his feed, I believe ; for he crawled like a slug.
But they were so taken up with discussing the
day's doings, and what a mort of people had been
present, and how the sheriff might have used
milder language in refusing my father, that they
forgot to use the whip.   The moon was up before
we got halfway home, and a star to be seen here
and there ; and still we never mended our pace.

'Twas in the middle of the lane leading down
to Hendra Bottom, where for more than a mile
two carts can't pass each other, that my father
pricks up his ears and looks back.

"Hullo!" says he; "there's somebody gallopin' behind us."

Far back in the night we heard the noise of a horse's hoofs, pounding furiously on the road and drawing nearer and nearer.

"Save us!" cries father; "whoever 'tis, he's comin' down th' lane!" And in a minute's time the clatter was close on us and someone shouting behind.

"Hurry that crawlin' worm o' yourn—or draw aside in God's name, an' let me by!" the rider yelled.

"What's up?" asked my father, quartering as well as he could. "Why! Hullo! Farmer Hugo, be that you?"

"There's a mad devil o' a man behind, ridin' down all he comes across. A 's blazin' drunk, I reckon—but 'tisn' *that*—'tis the horrible voice that goes wi' en—Hark! Lord protect us, he's turn'd into the lane!"

Sure enough, the clatter of a second horse was coming down upon us, out of the night— and with it the most ghastly sounds that ever creamed a man's flesh. Farmer Hugo pushed

past us and sent a shower of mud in our faces as
his horse leapt off again, and 'way-to-go down the
hill. My father stood up and lashed our old grey
with the reins, and down we went too, bumpity-
bump for our lives, the poor beast being taken
suddenly like one possessed. For the screaming
behind was like nothing on earth but the wailing
and sobbing of a little child—only tenfold
louder. 'Twas just as you'd fancy a baby might
wail if his little limbs was being twisted to
death.

At the hill's foot, as you know, a stream
crosses the lane—that widens out there a bit,
and narrows again as it goes up t'other side of
the valley. Knowing we must be overtaken
further on—for the screams and clatter seemed
at our very backs by this—father jumped out
here into the stream and backed the cart well
to one side ; and not a second too soon.

The next moment, like a wind, this thing
went by us in the moonlight—a man upon a
black horse that splashed the stream all over us
as he dashed through it and up the hill. 'Twas
the scarlet dragoon with his ashen face; and

behind him, holding to his cross-belt, rode a
little shape that tugged and wailed and raved.
As I stand here, sir, 'twas the shape of a naked
babe!

Well, I won't go on to tell how my father
dropped upon his knees in the water, or how my
mother fainted off. The thing was gone, and
from that moment for eight years nothing was
seen or heard of Sergeant Basket. The fright
killed my mother. Before next spring she fell
into a decline, and early next fall the old man—
for he was an old man now—had to delve her
grave. After this he went feebly about his
work, but held on, being wishful for me to step
into his shoon, which I began to do as soon as
I was fourteen, having outgrown the rickets by
that time.

But one cool evening in September month,
father was up digging in the yard alone: for
'twas a small child's grave, and in the loosest
soil, and I was off on a day's work, thatching
Farmer Tresidder's stacks. He was digging

away slowly when he heard a rattle at the lych-gate, and looking over the edge of the grave, saw in the dusk a man hitching his horse there by the bridle.

'Twas a coal-black horse, and the man wore a scarlet coat all powdered with pilm; and as he opened the gate and came over the graves, father saw that 'twas the dashing dragoon. His face was still a slaty-grey, and clammy with sweat; and when he spoke, his voice was all of a whisper, with a shiver therein.

"Bedman," says he, "go to the hedge and look down the road, and tell me what you see."

My father went, with his knees shaking, and came back again.

"I see a woman," says he, "not fifty yards down the road. She is dressed in black, an' has a veil over her face; an' she's comin' this way."

"Bedman," answers the dragoon, "go to the gate an' look back along the Plymouth road, an' tell me what you see."

"I see," says my father, coming back with

his teeth chattering, "I see, twenty yards back, a naked child comin'. He looks to be callin', but he makes no sound."

"Because his voice is wearied out," says the dragoon. And with that he faced about, and walked to the gate slowly.

"Bedman, come wi' me an' see the rest," he says, over his shoulder.

He opened the gate, unhitched the bridle and swung himself heavily up in the saddle.

Now from the gate the bank goes down pretty steep into the road, and at the foot of the bank my father saw two figures waiting. 'Twas the woman and the child, hand in hand ; and their eyes burned up like coals : and the woman's veil was lifted, and her throat bare.

As the horse went down the bank towards these two, they reached out and took each a stirrup and climbed upon his back, the child before the dragoon and the woman behind. The man's face was set like a stone. Not a word did either speak, and in this fashion they rode down the hill towards Ruan sands. All that my father could mind, beyond, was that the woman's hands were passed round the man's neck, where the rope had passed round her own.

No more could he tell, being a stricken man from that hour. But Aunt Polgrain, the housekeeper up to Constantine, saw them, an hour later, go along the road below the town-place ; and Jacobs, the smith, saw them pass his forge towards Bodmin about midnight. So the tale's true enough. But since that night no man has set eyes on horse or riders.

A BLUE PANTOMIME.

A BLUE PANTOMIME.

I.

HOW I DINED AT THE "INDIAN QUEENS."

THE sensation was odd; for I could have made affidavit I had never visited the place in my life, nor come within fifty miles of it. Yet every furlong of the drive was earmarked for me, as it were, by some detail perfectly familiar. The high-road ran straight ahead to a notch in the long chine of Huel Tor; and this notch was filled with the yellow ball of the westering sun. Whenever I turned my head and blinked, red simulacra of this ball hopped up and down over the brown moors. Miles of wasteland, dotted with peat-ricks and cropping ponies, stretched to the northern horizon: on our left three long coombes radiated seaward, and in the gorge of the midmost was a building stuck like a fish-bone, its twisted Jacobean chimneys overtopping a plantation of ash-trees that now, in November, allowed a glimpse, and no more, of the grey façade. I had looked down that coombe as we drove by; and catching sight of these chimneys felt something like reassurance, as if I had been counting, all the way, to find them there.

But here let me explain who I am and what brought me to these parts. My name is Samuel Wraxall—the Reverend Samuel Wraxall, to be precise: I was born a Cockney and educated at Rugby and Oxford. On leaving the University I had taken orders; but, for reasons impertinent to this narrative, was led, after five years of parochial work in Surrey, to accept an Inspectorship of Schools. Just now I was bound for Pitt's Scawens, a desolate village among the Cornish clay-moors, there to examine and report upon the Board School. Pitt's Scawens lies some nine miles off the railway, and six from the nearest market-town; consequently, on hearing there was a comfortable inn near the village, I had determined to make that my resting-place for the night and do my business early on the morrow.

"Who lives down yonder?" I asked my driver.

"Squire Parkyn," he answered, not troubling to follow my gaze.

"Old family?"

"May be: Belonged to these parts before I can mind."

"What's the place called?"

"Tremenhuel."

I had certainly never heard the name before, nevertheless my lips were forming the syllables almost before he spoke. As he flicked up his grey horse and the gig began to oscillate in more business-like fashion, I put him a fourth question—a question at once involuntary and absurd.

"Are you sure the people who live there are called Parkyn?"

He turned his head at this, and treated me quite excusably to a stare of amazement.

"Well—considerin' I've lived in these parts five-an'-forty year, man and boy, I reckon I *ought* to be sure."

The reproof was just, and I apologised.

Nevertheless Parkyn was not the name I wanted. What was the name? And why did I want it? I had not the least idea. For the next mile I continued to hunt my brain for the right combination of syllables. I only knew that somewhere, now at the back of my head, now on my tongue-tip, there hung a word I desired to utter, but could not. I was still searching for it when the gig climbed over the summit of a gentle rise, and the "Indian Queens" hove in sight.

It is not usual for a village to lie a full mile beyond its inn : yet I never doubted this must be the case with Pitt's Scawens. Nor was I in the least surprised by the appearance of this lonely tavern, with the black peat-pool behind it and the high-road in front, along which its end windows stare for miles, as if on the look-out for the ghosts of departed coaches full of disembodied travellers for the Land's End. I knew the sign-board over the porch : I knew— though now in the twilight it was impossible to distinguish colours—that upon either side of it was painted an Indian Queen in a scarlet turban and blue robe, taking two black children with scarlet parasols to see a blue palm-tree. I recognised the hepping-stock and granite drinking-trough beside the porch; as well as the eight front windows, four on either side of the door, and the dummy window immediately over it. Only the landlord was unfamiliar. He appeared as the gig drew up—a loose-fleshed, heavy man, something over six feet in height—and welcomed me with an air of anxious hospitality, as if I were the first guest he had entertained for many years.

"You received my letter, then?" I asked.

"Yes, surely. The Rev. S. Wraxall, I suppose. Your bed's aired, sir, and a fire in the Blue Room, and the cloth laid. My wife didn't like to risk cooking the fowl till you were really come. 'Railways be that uncertain,' she said. 'Something may happen to the train and he'll be done to death and all in pieces.'"

It took me a couple of seconds to discover that these gloomy anticipations referred not to me but to the fowl.

N

"But if you can wait half an hour——" he went on.

"Certainly," said I. "In the meanwhile, if you'll show me up to my bedroom, I'll have a wash and change my clothes, for I've been travelling since ten this morning."

I was standing in the passage by this time, and examined it in the dusk while the landlord was fetching a candle. Yes, again : I had felt sure the staircase lay to the right. I knew by heart the Ionic pattern of its broad balusters; the tick of the tall clock, standing at the first turn of the stairs; the vista down the glazed door opening on the stable-yard. When the landlord returned with my portmanteau and a candle and I followed him up-stairs, I was asking myself for the twentieth time—' When—in what stage of my soul's history—had I been doing all this before? And what on earth was that tune that kept humming in my head? '

I dismissed these speculations as I entered the bedroom and began to fling off my dusty clothes. I had almost forgotten about them by the time I began to wash away my travel-stains,

and rinse the coal-dust out of my hair. My
spirits revived, and I began mentally to arrange
my plans for the next day. The prospect of
dinner, too, after my cold drive was wonderfully
comforting. Perhaps (thought I), there is good
wine in this inn; it is just the house wherein
travellers find, or boast that they find, forgotten
bins of Burgundy or Teneriffe. When my landlord returned to conduct me to the Blue Room, I
followed him down to the first landing in the
lightest of spirits.

Therefore, I was startled when, as the
landlord threw open the door and stood aside
to let me pass, *it* came upon me again—and this
time not as a merely vague sensation, but as
a sharp and sudden fear taking me like a cold
hand by the throat. I shivered as I crossed the
threshold and began to look about me. The
landlord observed it, and said—

" It's chilly weather for travelling, to be
sure. Maybe you'd be better down-stairs in the
coffee-room, after all."

I felt that this was probable enough. But
it seemed a pity to have put him to the pains of

N 2

lighting this fire for nothing. So I promised him I should be comfortable enough.

He appeared to be relieved, and asked me what I would drink with my dinner. "There's beer—I brew it myself; and sherry——"

I said I would try his beer.

" And a bottle of sound port to follow ? "

Port upon home-brewed beer ! But I had dared it often enough in my Oxford days, and a long evening lay before me, with a snug arm-chair, and a fire fit to roast a sheep. I assented.

He withdrew to fetch up the meal, and I looked about me with curiosity. The room was a long one—perhaps fifty feet from end to end, and not less than ten paces broad. It was wainscotted to the height of four feet from the ground, probably with oak, but the wood had been so larded with dark blue paint that its texture could not be discovered. Above this wainscot the walls were covered with a fascinating paper. The background of this was a greenish-blue, and upon it a party of red-coated riders in three-cornered hats blew large horns while they hunted a stag. This pattern, striking

enough in itself, became immeasurably more so
when repeated a dozen times; for the stag of one
hunt chased the riders of the next, and the riders
chased the hounds, and so on in an unbroken
procession right round the room. The window
at the bottom of the room stood high in the
wall, with short blue curtains and a blue-
cushioned seat beneath. In the corner to the
right of it stood a tall clock, and by the clock an
old spinet, decorated with two plated cruets, a toy
cottage constructed of shells and gum, and an
ormolu clock under glass—the sort of ornament
that an Agricultural Society presents to the
tenant of the best-cultivated farm within thirty
miles of somewhere or other. The floor was uncarpeted save for one small oasis opposite the fire.
Here stood my table, cleanly spread, with two
plated candlesticks, each holding three candles.
Along the wainscot extended a regiment of dark,
leather-cushioned chairs, so straight in the back
that they seemed to be standing at attention.
There was but one easy-chair in the room, and
this was drawn close to the fire. I turned
towards it.

As I sat down I caught sight of my reflection in the mirror above the fireplace. It was an unflattering glass, with a wave across the surface that divided my face into two ill-fitting halves, and a film upon it, due, I suppose, to the smoke of the wood-fire below. But the setting of this mirror and the fireplace itself were by far the most noteworthy, objects in the whole room. I set myself idly to examine them.

It was an open hearth, and the blazing faggot lay on the stone itself. The andirons were of indifferently polished steel, and on either side of the fireplace two Ionic pilasters of dark oak supported a narrow mantel-ledge. Above this rested the mirror, flanked by a couple of naked, flat-cheeked boys, who appeared to be lowering it over the fire by a complicated system of pulleys, festoons, and flowers. These flowers and festoons, as well as the frame of the mirror, were of some light wood—lime, I fancy—and reminded me of Grinling Gibbons' work ; and the glass tilted forward at a surprising angle, as if about to tumble on the hearth-rug. The carving was exceedingly delicate. I rose to

examine it more narrowly. As I did so, my
eyes fell on three letters, cut in flowing italic
capitals upon a plain boss of wood immediately over the frame, and I spelt out the word
FVI.

Fui—the word was simple enough ; but
what of its associations ? Why should it begin
to stir up again those memories which were
memories of nothing? *Fui*—" I have been ";
but what the dickens have I been ?

The landlord came in with my dinner.

" Ah ! " said he, "you're looking at our
masterpiece, I see."

" Tell me," I asked ; " do you know why this
word is written here, over the mirror ? "

" I've heard my wife say, sir, it was the
motto of the Cardinnocks that used to own this
house. Ralph Cardinnock, father to the last
squire, built it. You'll see his initials up there,
in the top corners of the frame—R. C.—one
letter in each corner."

As he spoke it, I knew this name—Cardinnock—for that which had been haunting me.
I seated myself at table, saying—

"They lived at Tremenhuel, I suppose. Is the family gone?—died out?"

"Why yes; and the way of it was a bit curious, too."

"You might sit down and tell me about it," I said, "while I begin my dinner."

"There's not much to tell," he answered, taking a chair; "and I'm not the man to tell it properly. My wife is a better hand at it, but"—here he looked at me doubtfully—"it always makes her cry."

"Then I'd rather hear it from you. How did Tremenhuel come into the hands of the Parkyns?—that's the present owner's name, is it not?"

The landlord nodded. "The answer to that is part of the story. Old Parkyn, great-great-grandfather to the one that lives there now, took Tremenhuel on lease from the last Cardinnock—Squire Philip Cardinnock, as he was called. Squire Philip came into the property when he was twenty-three: and before he reached twenty-seven, he was forced to let the old place. He was wild, they say—thundering wild; a drinking, dicing, cock-fighting, horse-racing young man; poured out his money like water through a sieve. That was bad enough: but when it came to carrying off a young lady and putting a sword through her father and running the country, I put it to you it's worse."

" Did he disappear? "

" That's part of the story, too. When matters got desperate and he was forced to let Tremenhuel, he took what money he could raise and cleared out of the neighbourhood for a time; went off to Tregarrick when the militia was embodied, he being an officer; and there he cast his affections upon old Sir Felix Williams's daughter, Miss Cicely——"

I was expecting it: nevertheless I dropped my fork clumsily as I heard the name, and for a few seconds the landlord's voice sounded like that of a distant river as it ran on——

" And as Sir Felix wouldn't consent—for which nobody blamed him—Squire Philip and Miss Cicely agreed to go off together one dark night. But the old man found them out and stopped them in the nick of time and got six inches of cold steel for his pains. However, he kept his girl, and Squire Philip had to fly the country. He went off that same night, they say : and wherever he went, he never came back."

" What became of him ? "

" Ne'er a soul knows ; for ne'er a soul saw his face again. Year after year, old Parkyn, his tenant, took the rent of Tremenhuel out of his right pocket and paid it into his left : and in time, there being no heir, he just took over the property and stepped into Cardinnock's shoes with a ' by your leave ' to nobody, and there his grandson is to this day."

" What became of the young lady —of Miss Cicely Williams ? " I asked.

" Died an old maid. There was something curious between her and her only brother who had helped to stop the runaway match. Nobody knows what it was : but when Sir Felix died— as he did about ten years after—she packed up and went somewhere to the North of England and settled. They say she and her brother never spoke: which was carrying her anger at his interference rather far, 'specially as she remained good friends with her father."

He broke off here to fetch up the second course. We talked no more, for I was pondering his tale and disinclined to be diverted to other topics. Nor can I tell whether the rest of the meal was good or ill. I suppose I ate: but it was only when the landlord swept the cloth, and produced a bottle of port, with a plate of biscuits and another of dried raisins, that I woke out of my musing. While I drew the arm-chair nearer the fire, he pushed forward the table with the wine to my elbow. After this, he poured me out a glass and fell to dusting a high-backed chair with vigour, as though he had caught it standing at ease and were giving it a round dozen for insubordination in the ranks. "Was there anything more?" "Nothing, thank you." He withdrew.

I drank a couple of glasses and began meditatively to light my pipe. I was trying to piece together these words "Philip Cardinnock — Cicely Williams — *fui*," and to fit them into the tune that kept running in my head.

My pipe went out. I pulled out my pouch and was filling it afresh when a puff of wind came down the chimney and blew a cloud of blue smoke out into the room.

The smoke curled up and spread itself over the face of the mirror confronting me. I followed it lazily with my eyes. Then suddenly I bent forward, staring up. Something very curious was happening to the glass.

II.

WHAT I SAW IN THE MIRROR.

THE smoke that had dimmed the mirror's face for a moment was rolling off its surface and upwards to the ceiling. But some of it still lingered in filmy, slowly revolving eddies. The glass itself, too, was stirring beneath this film and running across its breadth in horizontal waves which broke themselves silently, one after another, against the dark frame, while the circles of smoke kept widening, as the ripples widen when a stone is tossed into still water.

I rubbed my eyes. The motion on the mirror's surface was quickening perceptibly, while the glass itself was steadily becoming more opaque, the film deepening to a milky colour and lying over the surface in heavy folds. I was about to start up and touch the glass with my hand, when beneath this milky colour and from the heart of the whirling film, there began to gleam an underlying brilliance after the fashion of the light in an opal, but with this difference, that the light here was blue—a steel blue so vivid that the pain of it forced me to shut my eyes. When I opened them again, this light had increased in intensity. The disturbance in the glass began to abate; the eddies revolved more slowly; the smoke-wreaths faded: and as they died wholly out, the blue light went out on a sudden and the mirror looked down upon me as before.

That is to say, I thought so for a moment. But the next, I found that though its face reflected the room in which I sat, there was one omission.

I was that omission. My arm-chair was there, but no one sat in it.

I was surprised; but, as well as I can recollect, not in the least frightened. I continued, at any rate, to gaze steadily into the glass, and now took note of two particulars that had escaped me. The table I saw was laid for two. Forks, knives and glasses gleamed at either end, and a couple of decanters caught the sparkle of

the candles in the centre. This was my first
observation. The second was that the colours
of the hearth-rug had gained in freshness, and
that a dark spot just beyond it—a spot which in
my first exploration I had half-amusedly taken
for a blood-stain—was not reflected in the glass.

As I leant back and gazed, with my hands
in my lap, I remember there was some difficulty
in determining whether the tune by which I
was still haunted ran in my head or was tinkling
from within the old spinet by the window. But
after a while the music, whencesoever it came,
faded away and ceased. A dead silence held
everything for about thirty seconds.

And then, still looking in the mirror, I saw
the door behind me open slowly.

The next moment, two persons noiselessly
entered the room—a young man and a girl.
They wore the dress of the early Georgian days,
as well as I could see ; for the girl was wrapped
in a cloak with a hood that almost concealed her
face, while the man wore a heavy riding-coat.
He was booted and spurred, and the backs of
his top-boots were splashed with mud. I say

the backs of his boots, for he stood with his
back to me while he held open the door for the
girl to pass, and at first I could not see his face.

The lady advanced into the light of the
candles and threw back her hood. Her eyes
were dark and frightened: her cheeks damp with
rain and slightly reddened by the wind. A curl
of brown hair had broken loose from its knot
and hung, heavy with wet, across her brow. It
was a beautiful face; and I recognised its owner.
She was Cicely Williams.

With that, I knew well enough what I was
to see next. I knew it even while the man at
the door was turning, and I dug the nails of my
right hand into the palm of my left, to repress
the fear that swelled up as a wave as I looked
straight into his face and saw—*my own self*.

But I had expected it, as I say: and when
the wave of fear had passed over me and gone,
I could observe these two figures steadfastly
enough. The girl dropped into a chair beside
the table, and stretching her arms along the
white cloth, bowed her head over them and
wept. I saw her shoulders heave and her

twined fingers work as she struggled with her grief. The young Squire advanced and, with a hand on her shoulder, endeavoured by many endearments to comfort her. His lips moved vehemently, and gradually her shoulders ceased to rise and fall. By-and-by she raised her head and looked up into his face with wet, gleaming eyes. It was very pitiful to see. The young man took her face between his hands, kissed it, and pouring out a glass of wine, held it to her lips. She put it aside with her hand and glanced up towards the tall clock in the corner. My eyes, following hers, saw that the hands pointed to a quarter to twelve.

The young Squire set down the glass hastily, stepped to the window and, drawing aside the blue curtain, gazed out upon the night. Twice he looked back at Cicely, over his shoulder, and after a minute returned to the table. He drained the glass which the girl had declined, poured out another, still keeping his eyes on her, and began to walk impatiently up and down the room. And all the time Cicely's soft eyes never ceased to follow him. Clearly there was

o

need for hurry, for they had not laid aside
their travelling-cloaks, and once or twice the
young man paused in his walk to listen. At
length he pulled out his watch, glanced from it
to the clock in the corner, put it away with a
frown and, striding up to the hearth, flung himself down in the arm-chair—the very arm-chair
in which I was seated.

As he sat there, tapping the hearth-rug
with the toe of his thick riding-boot and moving
his lips now and then in answer to some question from the young girl, I had time to examine
his every feature. Line by line they reproduced
my own—nay, looking straight into his eyes I
could see through them into the soul of him
and recognised that soul for my own. Of all the
passions there I knew that myself contained the
germs. Vices repressed in youth, tendencies to sin
starved in my own nature by lack of opportunity
—these flourished in a rank growth. I saw
virtues, too, that I had once possessed but had
lost by degrees in my respectable journey through
life—courage, generosity, tenderness of heart.
I was discovering these with envy, one by one,

when he raised his head higher and listened for a moment, with a hand on either arm of the chair.

The next instant he sprang up and faced the door. Glancing at Cicely, I saw her cowering down in her chair.

The young Squire had hardly gained his feet when the door flew open and the figures of two men appeared on the threshold—Sir Felix Williams and his only son, the father and brother of Cicely.

There, in the doorway, the intruders halted; but for an instant only. Almost before the Squire could draw, his sweetheart's brother had sprung forward. Like two serpents their rapiers engaged in the candle-light. The soundless blades crossed and glittered. Then one of them flickered in a narrow circle, and the brother's rapier went spinning from his hand across the room.

Young Cardinnock lowered his point at once, and his adversary stepped back a couple of paces. While a man might count twenty the pair looked each other in the face, and then the old man, Sir Felix, stepped slowly forward.

o 2

But before he could thrust—for the young Squire still kept his point lowered—Cicely sprang forward and threw herself across her lover's breast. There, for all the gentle efforts his left hand made to disengage her, she clung. She had made her choice. There was no sign of faltering in her soft eyes, and her father had perforce to hold his hand.

The old man began to speak. I saw his face distorted with passion and his lips working. I saw the deep red gather on Cicely's cheeks and the anger in her lover's eyes. There was a pause as Sir Felix ceased to speak, and then the young Squire replied. But his sentence stopped midway : for once more the old man rushed upon him.

This time young Cardinnock's rapier was raised. Girdling Cicely with his left arm he parried her father's lunge and smote his blade aside. But such was the old man's passion that he followed the lunge with all his body, and before his opponent could prevent it, was wounded high in the chest, beneath the collar-bone.

He reeled back and fell against the table.

Cicely ran forward and caught his hand; but he pushed her away savagely and, with another clutch at the table's edge, dropped upon the hearth-rug. The young man, meanwhile, white and aghast, rushed to the table, filled a glass with wine, and held it to the lips of the wounded man. So the two lovers knelt.

It was at this point that I who sat and witnessed the tragedy was assailed by a horror entirely new. Hitherto I had, indeed, seen myself in Squire Philip Cardinnock; but now I began also to possess his soul and feel with his feelings, while at the same time I continued to sit before the glass, a helpless onlooker. I was two men at once; the man who knelt all unaware of what was coming and the man who waited in the arm-chair, incapable of word or movement, yet gifted with a torturing pre-science. And as I sat this was what I saw:—

The brother, as I knelt there oblivious of all but the wounded man, stepped across the room to the corner where his rapier lay, picked it up softly and as softly stole up behind me. I tried to shout, to warn myself; but my tongue was tied. The brother's arm was lifted. The candle-light ran along the blade. Still the kneeling figure never turned.

And as my heart stiffened and awaited it, there came a flash of pain—one red-hot stroke of anguish.

III.

WHAT I SAW IN THE TARN.

As the steel entered my back, cutting all the cords that bound me to life, I suffered anguish too exquisite for words to reach, too deep for memory to dive after. My eyes closed and teeth shut on the taste of death; and as they shut a merciful oblivion wrapped me round.

When I awoke, the room was dark, and I was standing on my feet. A cold wind was blowing on my face, as from an open door. I staggered to meet this wind and found myself groping along a passage and down a staircase filled with Egyptian darkness. Then the wind increased suddenly and shook the black curtain around my senses. A murky light broke in on me. I had a body. That I felt; but where it was I knew not. And so I felt my way forward in the direction where the twilight showed least dimly.

Slowly the curtain shook and its folds dis-
solved as I moved against the wind. The clouds
lifted; and by degrees I grew aware that I
was standing on the barren moor. Night was
stretched around to the horizon, where straight
ahead a grey bar shone across the gloom. I
pressed on towards it. The heath was uneven
under my feet, and now and then I stumbled
heavily; but still I held on. For it seemed
that I must get to this grey bar or die a second
time. All my muscles, all my will, were
strained upon this purpose.

Drawing nearer, I observed that a wave-like
motion kept passing over this brighter space, as
it had passed over the mirror. The glimmer
would be obscured for a moment, and then re-
appear. At length a gentle acclivity of the
moor hid it for a while. My legs positively
raced up this slope, and upon the summit I
hardly dared to look for a moment, knowing
that if the light were an illusion all my hope
must die with it.

But it was no illusion. There was the light,
and there, before my feet, lay a sable sheet of

water, over the surface of which the light was playing. There was no moon, no star in heaven; yet over this desolate tarn hovered a pale radiance that ceased again where the edge of its waves lapped the further bank of peat. Their monotonous wash hardly broke the stillness of the place.

The formless longing was now pulling at me with an attraction I could not deny, though within me there rose and fought against it a horror only less strong. Here, as in the Blue Room, two souls were struggling for me. It was the soul of Philip Cardinnock that drew me towards the tarn and the soul of Samuel Wraxall that resisted. Only, what was the thing towards which I was being pulled?

I must have stood at least a minute on the brink before I descried a black object floating at the far end of the tarn. What this object was I could not make out; but I knew it on the instant to be that for which I longed, and all my will grew suddenly intent on drawing it nearer. Even as my volition centred upon it, the black spot began to move slowly out into the pale radiance towards me. Silently, surely, as though my wish drew it by a rope, it floated nearer and nearer over the bosom of the tarn; and while it was still some twenty yards from me I saw it to be a long black box, shaped somewhat like a coffin.

There was no doubt about it. I could hear the water now sucking at its dark sides. I stepped down the bank, and waded up to my knees in the icy water to meet it. It was a plain box, with no writing upon the lid, nor any speck of metal to relieve the dead black: and it moved with the same even speed straight up to where I stood.

As it came, I laid my hand upon it and touched wood. But with the touch came a further sensation that made me fling both arms around the box and begin frantically to haul it towards the shore.

It was a feeling of suffocation; of a weight that pressed in upon my ribs and choked the lungs' action. I felt that I must open that box or die horribly; that until I had it upon the bank and had forced the lid up I should know no pause from the labour and torture of dying.

This put a wild strength into me. As the box grated upon the few pebbles by the shore, I bent over it, caught it once more by the sides, and with infinite effort dragged it up out of the water. It was heavy, and the weight upon my chest was heavier yet : but straining, panting, gasping, I hauled it up the bank, dropped it on the turf, and knelt over it, tugging furiously at the lid.

I was frenzied—no less. My nails were torn until the blood gushed. Lights danced before me; bells rang in my ears; the pressure on my lungs grew more intolerable with each moment; but still I fought with that lid. Seven devils were within me and helped me ; and all the while I knew that I was dying, that unless the box were opened in a moment or two it would be too late.

The sweat ran off my eyebrows and dripped on the box. My breath came and went in sobs. I could not die. I could not, must not die. And so I tugged and strained and tugged again.

Then, as I felt the black anguish of the Blue Room descending a second time upon me, I seemed to put all my strength into my hands. From the lid or from my own throat—I could not distinguish—there came a creak and a long groan. I tore back the board and fell on the heath with one shuddering breath of relief.

And drawing it, I raised my head and looked over the coffin's edge. Still drawing it, I tumbled back.

White, cold, with the last struggle fixed on its features and open eyes, it was my own dead face that stared up at me!

IV.

WHAT I HAVE SINCE LEARNT.

THEY found me, next morning, lying on the brink of the tarn, and carried me back to the inn. There I lay for weeks in a brain fever and talked—as they assure me—the wildest nonsense. The landlord had first guessed that something was amiss on finding the front door open when he came down at five o'clock. I must have turned to the left on leaving the house, travelled up the road for a hundred yards, and then struck almost at right angles across the moor. One of my shoes was found a furlong from the highway, and this had guided them. Of course they found no coffin beside me, and I was prudent enough to hold my tongue when I became convalescent. But the effect of that night was to shatter my health for a year and more, and force me to throw up my post of School Inspector. To this day I have never examined the school at Pitt's Scawens. But somebody else has ; and last winter I received a letter, which I will give in full :—

21, CHESTERHAM ROAD, KENSINGTON, W.
December 3rd, 1891.

DEAR WRAXALL,—

It is a long time since we have corresponded, but I have just returned from Cornwall, and while visiting Pitt's Scawens professionally, was reminded of you. I put up at the inn where you had your long illness. The people there were delighted to find that I knew you, and desired me to send "their duty" when next I wrote. By the way, I suppose you were introduced to their state apartment— the Blue Room—and its wonderful chimney carving. I made a bid to the landlord for it, panels, mirror, and all, but he referred me to Squire Parkyn, the landlord. I think I may get it, as the Squire loves hard coin. When I have it up over my mantel-piece here you must run over and give me your opinion on it. By the way, clay has been discovered on the Tremenhuel Estate, just at the back of the "Indian Queens": at least, I hear that Squire Parkyn is running a Company, and is sanguine. You remember the tarn behind the inn? They made an odd discovery there when draining it for the new works. In the mud at the bottom was imbedded the perfect skeleton of a man. The bones were quite clean and white. Close beside the body they afterwards turned up a silver snuff-box, with the word " Fui " on the lid. " Fui " was the motto of the Cardinnocks, who held Tremenhuel before it passed to the Parkyns. There seems to be no doubt that these are the bones of the last Squire, who disappeared mysteriously more than a hundred years ago, in consequence of a love affair, I'm told. It looks like foul play ; but, if so, the account has long since passed out of the hands of man.

Yours ever,   DAVID E. MAINWARING.

P.S.—I reopen this to say that Squire Parkyn has accepted my offer for the chimney-piece. Let me hear soon that you'll come and look at it and give me your opinion.

THE TWO HOUSEHOLDERS.

THE
TWO HOUSEHOLDERS.

Extract from the Memoirs of Gabriel Foot,
Highwayman.

I WILL say this—speaking as accurately as a man may, so long afterwards—that when first I spied the house it put no desire in me but just to give thanks.

For conceive my case. It was near midnight, and ever since dusk I had been tramping the naked moors, in the teeth of as vicious a nor'-wester as ever drenched a man to the skin, and then blew the cold home to his marrow. My clothes were sodden; my coat-tails flapped with a noise like pistol-shots; my boots squeaked as I went. Overhead, the October moon was in her last quarter, and might have been a slice of finger-nail for all the light she afforded. Two-thirds of the time the wrack blotted her out altogether; and I, with my stick clipped tight under my armpit, eyes puckered up, and head bent aslant, had to keep my wits alive to distinguish the road from the black heath to right and left. For three hours I had met neither man nor man's dwelling, and (for all I knew) was desperately lost. , Indeed, at the cross-roads, two miles back, there had been nothing for me but to choose the way that kept the wind on my face, and it gnawed me like a dog.

Mainly to allay the stinging of my eyes, I pulled up at last, turned right-about-face, leant back against the blast with a hand on my hat, and surveyed the blackness behind. It was at this instant that, far away to the left, a point of light caught my notice, faint but steady; and at once I felt sure it burnt in the window of a house. "The house," thought I, "is a good mile off, beside the other road, and the light must have been an inch over my hat-brim for the last half-hour." This reflection— that on so wide a moor I had come near missing the information I wanted (and perhaps a supper) by one inch—sent a strong thrill down my back.

I cut straight across the heather towards the light, risking quags and pitfalls. Nay, so heartening was the chance to hear a fellow creature's voice, that I broke into a run, skipping over the stunted gorse that cropped up here and there, and dreading every moment to see the light quenched. " Suppose it burns in an upper window, and the family is going to bed, as would be likely at this hour——" The apprehension kept my eyes fixed on the bright spot, to the frequent scandal of my legs, that within five minutes were stuck full of gorse prickles.

But the light did not go out, and soon a flicker of moonlight gave me a glimpse of the house's outline. It proved to be a deal more imposing than I looked for—the outline, in fact, of a tall, square barrack, with a cluster of chimneys at either end, like ears, and a high wall, topped by the roofs of some outbuildings, concealing the lower windows. There was no gate in this wall, and presently I guessed the reason. I was approaching the place from behind, and the light came from a back window on the first floor.

The faintness of the light also was explained by this time. It shone behind a drab-coloured blind, and in shape resembled the stem of a wine-glass, broadening out at the foot; an effect produced by the half-drawn curtains within. I came to a halt, waiting for the next ray of moonlight. At the same moment a rush of wind swept over the chimney-stacks, and on the wind there seemed to ride a human sigh.

On this last point I may err. The gust had passed some seconds before I caught myself detecting this peculiar note, and trying to disengage it from the natural chords of the storm. From the next gust it was absent; and then, to my dismay, the light faded from the window.

I was half-minded to call out when it appeared again, this time in two windows—those next on the right to that where it had shone before. Almost at once it increased in brilliance, as if the person who carried it from the smaller room to the larger were lighting more candles; and now the illumination was strong enough to make fine gold threads of the rain that fell within its radiance, and fling two shafts of warm yellow over the coping of the back wall. During the minute or more that I stood watching, no shadow fell on either blind.

Between me and the wall ran a ditch, into which the ground at my feet broke sharply away. Setting my back to the storm again, I followed the lip of this ditch around the wall's angle. Here it shallowed, and here, too, was shelter; but not wishing to mistake a bed of nettles or any such pitfall for solid earth, I kept pretty wide as I went on. The house was dark on this side, and the wall, as before, had no opening. Close beside the next angle there grew a mass of thick gorse bushes, and pushing through these I found myself suddenly on a sound high-road, with the wind tearing at me as furiously as ever.

But here was the front; and I now perceived that the surrounding wall advanced some way before the house, so as to form a narrow courtlage. So much of it, too, as faced the road had been whitewashed, which made it an easy matter to find the gate. But as I laid hand on its latch I had a surprise.

A line of paving-stones led from the gate to a heavy porch; and along the wet surface of these there fell a streak of light from the front door, which stood ajar.

That a door should remain six inches open on such a night was astonishing enough, until I entered the court and found it as still as a room, owing to the high wall. But looking up and assuring myself that all the rest of the façade was black as ink, I wondered at the carelessness of the inmates.

It was here that my professional instinct received the first jog. Abating the sound of my feet on the paving-stones, I went up to the door and pushed it softly. It opened without noise.

I stepped into a fair-sized hall of modern build, paved with red tiles and lit with a small hanging-lamp. To right and left were doors leading to the ground-floor rooms. Along the

wall by my shoulder ran a line of pegs, on which
hung half-a-dozen hats and great-coats, every
one of clerical shape; and full in front of me
a-broad staircase ran up, with a staring Brussels
carpet, the colours and pattern of which I can
recall as well as I can to-day's breakfast.
Under this staircase was set a stand full of
walking-sticks, and a table littered with gloves,
brushes, a hand-bell, a riding-crop, one or two
dog-whistles, and a bedroom candle, with tinder-
box beside it. This, with one notable exception,
was all the furniture.

The exception—which turned me cold—was
the form of a yellow mastiff dog, curled on a
mat beneath the table. The arch of his back
was towards me, and one forepaw lay over his
nose in a natural posture of sleep. I leant back
on the wainscotting with my eyes tightly fixed
on him, and my thoughts sneaking back, with
something of regret, to the storm I had come
through.

But a man's habits are not easily denied.
At the end of three minutes the dog had not
moved, and I was down on the door-mat unlacing

my soaked boots. Slipping them off, and taking them in my left hand, I stood up, and tried a step towards the stairs, with eyes alert for any movement of the mastiff; but he never stirred. I was glad enough, however, on reaching the stairs, to find them newly built, and the carpet thick. Up I went, with a glance at every step for the table which now hid the brute's form from me, and never a creak did I wake out of that staircase till I was almost at the first landing, when my toe caught a loose stair-rod, and rattled it in a way that stopped my heart for a moment, and then set it going in double-quick time.

I stood still with a hand on the rail. My eyes were now on a level with the floor of the landing, out of which branched two passages— one turning sharply to my right, the other straight in front, so that I was gazing down the length of it. Almost at the end, a parallelogram of light fell across it from an open door.

A man who has once felt it knows there is only one kind of silence that can fitly be called "dead." This is only to be found in a

great house at midnight. I declare that for a
few seconds after I rattled the stair-rod you
might have cut the silence with a knife. If
the house held a clock, it ticked inaudibly.

Upon this silence, at the end of a minute,
broke a light sound—the *tink-tink* of a decanter
on the rim of a wine-glass. It came from the
room where the light was.

Now perhaps it was that the very thought
of liquor put warmth into my cold bones. It is
certain that all of a sudden I straightened my
back, took the remaining stairs at two strides,
and walked down the passage as bold as brass,
without caring a jot for the noise I made.

In the doorway I halted. The room was
long, lined for the most part with books bound
in what they call "divinity calf," and littered
with papers like a barrister's table on assize day.
A leathern elbow-chair faced the fireplace, where
a few coals burned sulkily, and beside it, on the
corner of a writing table, were set an unlit
candle and a pile of manuscripts. At the opposite end of the room a curtained door led (as I
guessed) to the chamber that I had first seen

illuminated. All this I took in with the tail of
my eye, while staring straight in front, where,
in the middle of a great square of carpet,
between me and the windows, stood a table with
a red cloth upon it. On this cloth were a
couple of wax candles lit, in silver stands, a tray,
and a decanter three-parts full of brandy. And
between me and the table stood a man.

He stood sideways, leaning a little back, as
if to keep his shadow off the threshold, and
looked at me over his left shoulder—a bald,
grave man, slightly under the common height,
with a long clerical coat of preposterous fit
hanging loosely from his shoulders, a white
cravat, black breeches, and black stockings.
His feet were loosely thrust into carpet slip-
pers. I judged his age at fifty, or thereabouts; but his face rested in the shadow,
and I could only note a pair of eyes, very
small and alert, twinkling above a large ex-
panse of cheek.

He was lifting a wine-glass from the table at
the moment when I appeared, and it trembled
now in his right hand. I heard a spilt drop

or two fall on the carpet. This was all the evidence he showed of discomposure.

Setting the glass back, he felt in his breast-pocket for a handkerchief, failed to find one, and rubbed his hands together to get the liquor off his fingers.

"You startled me," he said, in a matter-of-fact tone, turning his eyes upon me, as he lifted his glass again, and emptied it. "How did you find your way in?"

"By the front door," said I, wondering at his unconcern.

He nodded his head slowly.

"Ah! yes; I forgot to lock it. You came to steal, I suppose?"

"I came because I'd lost my way. I've been travelling this God-forsaken moor since dusk——"

"With your boots in your hand," he put in quietly.

"I took them off out of respect to the yellow dog you keep."

"He lies in a very natural attitude—eh?"

"You don't tell me he was *stuffed?*"

The old man's eyes beamed a contemptuous pity.

" You are indifferent sharp, my dear sir, for a housebreaker. Come in. Set down those convicting boots, and don't drip pools of water in the doorway. If I must entertain a burglar, I prefer him tidy."

He walked to the fire, picked up a poker, and knocked the coals into a blaze. This done, he turned round on me with the poker still in his hand. The serenest gravity sat on his large, pale features.

" Why have I done this ? " he asked.

" I suppose to get possession of the poker."

" Quite right.   May I inquire your next move ? "

" Why ? " said I, feeling in my tail-pocket, " I carry a pistol."

" Which I suppose to be damp ? "

" By no means.   I carry it, as you see, in an oil-cloth case."

He stooped, and laid the poker carefully in the fender.

" That is a stronger card than I possess.   I

might urge that by pulling the trigger you would certainly alarm the house and the neighbourhood, and put a halter round your neck. But it strikes me as safer to assume you capable of using a pistol with effect at three paces. With what might happen subsequently I will not pretend to be concerned. The fate of your neck " — he waved a hand, — " well, I have known you for just five minutes, and feel but a moderate interest in your neck. As for the inmates of this house, it will refresh you to hear that there are none. I have lived here two years with a butler and female cook, both of whom I dismissed yesterday at a minute's notice, for conduct which I will not shock your ears by explicitly naming. Suffice it to say, I carried them off yesterday to my parish church, two miles away, married them and dismissed them in the vestry without characters. I wish you had known that butler—but excuse me; with the information I have supplied, you ought to find no difficulty in fixing the price you will take to clear out of my house instanter."

"Sir," I answered, "I have held a pistol at one or two heads in my time, but never at one stuffed with nobler indiscretion. Your chivalry does not, indeed, disarm me, but prompts me to desire more of your acquaintance. I have found a gentleman, and must sup with him before I make terms."

This address seemed to please him. He shuffled across the room to a sideboard, and produced a plate of biscuits, another of dried figs, a glass, and two decanters.

"Sherry and Madeira," he said. "There is also a cold pie in the larder, if you care for it."

"A biscuit will serve," I replied. "To tell the truth, I'm more for the bucket than the manger, as the grooms say : and the brandy you were tasting just now is more to my mind than wine."

"There is no water handy."

"I have soaked in enough to-night to last me with this bottle."

I pulled over a chair, laid my pistol on the table, and held out the glass for him to fill.

Having done so, he helped himself to a glass and a chair, and sat down facing me.

"I was speaking, just now, of my late butler," he began, with a sip at his brandy. "Does it strike you that, when confronted with moral delinquency, I am apt to let my indignation get the better of me?"

"Not at all," I answered heartily, refilling my glass.

It appeared that another reply would have pleased him better.

"H'm. I was hoping that, perhaps, I had visited his offence too strongly. As a clergyman, you see, I was bound to be severe; but upon my word, sir, since Parkinson left I have felt like a man who has lost a limb."

He drummed with his fingers on the cloth for a few moments, and went on—

"One has a natural disposition to forgive butlers—Pharaoh, for instance, felt it. There hovers around butlers an atmosphere in which common ethics lose their pertinence. But mine was a rare bird—a black swan among butlers! He was more than a butler: he was a quick

Q

and brightly gifted man. Of the accuracy of his taste, and the unusual scope of his endeavour, you will be able to form some opinion when I assure you he modelled himself upon *me*."

I bowed, over my brandy.

"I am a scholar: yet I employed him to read aloud to me, and derived pleasure from his intonation. I talk with refinement: yet he learned to answer me in language as precise as my own. My cast-off garments fitted him not more irreproachably than did my amenities of manner. Divest him of his tray, and you would find his mode of entering a room hardly distinguishable from my own—the same urbanity, the same alertness of carriage, the same superfine deference towards the weaker sex. All—all my idiosyncrasies I saw reflected in him; and can you doubt that I was gratified? He was my *alter ego*—which, by the way, makes it harder for me to pardon his behaviour with the cook."

"Look here," I broke in; "you want a new butler?"

" Oh, you really grasp that fact, do you? " he retorted.

" Why, then," said I, " let me cease to be your burglar and let me continue here as your butler."

He leant back, spreading out the fingers of each hand on the table's edge.

" Believe me," I went on, "you might do worse. I have been in my time a demy of Magdalen College, Oxford, and retain some Greek and Latin. I'll undertake to read the Fathers with an accent that shall not offend you. My taste in wine is none the worse for having been formed in other men's cellars. Moreover, you shall engage the ugliest cook in Christendom, so long as I'm your butler. I've taken a liking to you—that's flat—and I apply for the post."

" I give forty pounds a year," said he.

" And I'm cheap at that price."

He filled up his glass, looking up at me while he did so with the air of one digesting a problem. From first to last his face was grave as a judge's.

Q 2

"We are too impulsive, I think," was his answer, after a minute's silence; "and your speech smacks of the amateur. You say, 'Let me cease to be your burglar and let me be your butler.' The aspiration is respectable; but a man might as well say, 'Let me cease to write sermons, let me paint pictures.' And truly, sir, you impress me as no expert even in your present trade."

"On the other hand," I argued, "consider the moderation of my demands; that alone should convince you of my desire to turn over a new leaf. I ask for a month's trial; if at the end of that time I don't suit, you shall say so, and I'll march from your door with nothing in my pocket but my month's wages. Be hanged, sir! but when I reflect on the amount you'll have to pay to get me to face to-night's storm again, you seem to be getting off dirt cheap!" cried I, slapping my palm on the table.

"Ah, if you had only known Parkinson!" he exclaimed.

Now the third glass of clean spirit has

always a deplorable effect on me. It turns me from bright to black, from levity to extreme sulkiness. I have done more wickedness over this third tumbler than in all the other states of comparative inebriety within my experience. So now I glowered at my companion and cursed.

" Look here, I don't want to hear any more of Parkinson, and I've a pretty clear notion of the game you're playing. You want to make me drink, and you're ready to sit prattling there plying me till I drop under the table."

" Do me the favour to remember that you came, and are staying, on your own motion. As for the brandy, I would remind you that I suggested a milder drink. Try some Madeira."

He handed me the decanter, as he spoke, and I poured out a glass.

" Madeira ! " said I, taking a gulp, " Ugh ! it's the commonest Marsala ! "

I had no sooner said the words than he rose up, and stretched a hand gravely across to me.

" I hope you will shake it," he said ; " though, as a man who after three glasses of neat spirit can distinguish between Madeira and

Marsala, you have every right to refuse me. Two minutes ago you offered to become my butler, and I demurred. I now beg you to repeat that offer. Say the word, and I employ you gladly: you shall even have the second decanter (which contains genuine Madeira) to take to bed with you."

We shook hands on our bargain, and catching up a candlestick, he led the way from the room.

Picking up my boots, I followed him along the passage and down the silent staircase. In the hall he paused to stand on tip-toe, and turn up the lamp, which was burning low. As he did so, I found time to fling a glance at my old enemy, the mastiff. He lay as I had first seen him—a stuffed dog, if ever there was one. "Decidedly," thought I, "my wits are to seek to-night;" and with the same, a sudden suspicion made me turn to my conductor, who had advanced to the left-hand door, and was waiting for me, with a hand on the knob.

"One moment!" I said: "This is all very pretty, but how am I to know you're not sending me to bed while you fetch in all the countryside to lay me by the heels ? "

" I'm afraid," was his answer, " you must be content with my word, as a gentleman, that never, to-night or hereafter, will I breathe a syllable about the circumstances of your visit. However, if you choose, we will return up-stairs."

" No ; I'll trust you," said I ; and he opened the door.

It led into a broad passage paved with slate, upon which three or four rooms opened. He paused by the second and ushered me into a sleeping-chamber, which, though narrow, was comfortable enough—a vast improvement, at any rate, on the mumpers' lodgings I had been used to for many months past.

" You can undress here," he said. " The sheets are aired, and if you'll wait a moment, I'll fetch a nightshirt—one of my own."

" Sir, you heap coals of fire on me."

" Believe me that for ninety-nine of your qualities I do not care a tinker's curse ; but for your palate you are to be taken care of."

He shuffled away, but came back in a couple of minutes with the nightshirt.

"Good-night," he called to me, flinging it in at the door; and without giving me time to return the wish, went his way up-stairs.

Now it might be supposed I was only too glad to toss off my clothes and climb into the bed I had so unexpectedly acquired a right to. But, as a matter of fact, I did nothing of the kind. Instead, I drew on my boots and sat on the bed's edge, blinking at my candle till it died down in its socket, and afterwards at the purple square of window as it slowly changed to grey with the coming of dawn. I was cold to the heart, and my teeth chattered with an ague. Certainly I never suspected my host's word; but was even occupied in framing good resolutions and, shaping out a reputable future, when I heard the front door gently pulled to, and a man's footsteps moving quietly to the gate.

The treachery knocked me in a heap for the moment. Then, leaping up and flinging my door wide, I stumbled through the uncertain light of the passage into the front hall.

There was a fan-shaped light over the door, and the place was very still and grey. A quick thought, or, rather, a sudden, prophetic guess at the truth, made me turn to the figure of the mastiff curled under the hall table.

I laid my hand on the scruff of his neck. He was quite limp, and my fingers sank into the flesh on either side of the vertebræ. Digging them deeper, I dragged him out into the middle of the hall and pulled the front door open to see the better.

His throat was gashed from ear to ear.

How many seconds passed after I dropped the senseless lump on the floor, and before I made another movement, it would puzzle me to say. Twice I stirred a foot as if to run out at the door. Then, changing my mind, I stepped over the mastiff, and ran up the staircase.

The passage at the top was now dark ; but groping down it, I found the study door open, as before, and passed in. A sick light stole through the blinds—enough for me to distinguish the glasses and decanters on the table, and find my way to the curtain that hung before the inner room.

I pushed the curtain aside, paused for a moment, and listened to the violent beat of my heart; then felt for the door-handle and turned it.

All I could see at first was that the chamber was small; next, that the light patch in a line with the window was the white coverlet of a bed; and next that somebody, or something, lay on the bed.

I listened again. There was no sound in the room; no heart beating but my own. I reached out a hand to pull up the blind, and drew it back again. I dared not.

The daylight grew minute by minute on the dull oblong of the blind, and minute by minute that horrible thing on the bed took something of distinctness.

The strain beat me at last. I fetched a loud yell to give myself courage, and, reaching for the cord, pulled up the blind as fast as it would go.

The face on the pillow was that of an old

man—a face waxen and peaceful, with quiet lines about the mouth and eyes, and long lines of grey hair falling back from the temples. The body was turned a little on one side, and one hand lay outside the bedclothes in a very natural manner. But there were two big dark stains on the pillow and coverlet.

Then I knew I was face to face with the real householder, and it flashed on me that I had been indiscreet in taking service as his butler, and that I knew the face his ex-butler wore.

And, being by this time awake to the responsibilities of the post, I quitted it three steps at a time, not once looking behind me. Outside the house the storm had died down, and white daylight was gleaming over the sodden moors. But my bones were cold, and I ran faster and faster.

THE DISENCHANTMENT OF
'LIZABETH.

THE
DISENCHANTMENT OF 'LIZABETH.

" So you reckon I've got to die? "

The room was mean, but not without
distinction. The meanness lay in lime-washed
walls, scant fittings, and uncovered boards;
the distinction came of ample proportions
and something of durability in the furniture.
Rooms, like human faces, reflect their histories;
and that generation after generation of the same
family had here struggled to birth or death was
written in this chamber unmistakably. The
candle-light, twinkling on the face of a dark
wardrobe near the door, lit up its rough in-
scription, "S.T. and M.T., MDCLXVII"; the
straight-backed oaken chairs might well claim
an equal age; and the bed in the corner was

a spacious four-poster, pillared in smooth mahogany and curtained in faded green damask.

In the shadow of this bed lay the man who had spoken. A single candle stood on a tall chest at his left hand, and its ray, filtering through the thin green curtain, emphasised the hue of death on his face. The features were pinched, and very old. His tone held neither complaint nor passion : it was matter-of-fact even, as of one whose talk is merely a concession to good manners. There was the faintest interrogation in it; no more.

After a minute or so, getting no reply, he added more querulously—

" I reckon you might answer, 'Lizabeth. Do'ee think I've got to die ? "

'Lizabeth, who stood by the uncurtained window, staring into the blackness without, barely turned her head to answer—

" Certain."

" Doctor said so, did he ? "

'Lizabeth, still with her back towards him, nodded. For a minute or two there was silence.

" I don't feel like dyin'; but doctor ought to

know. Seemed to me 'twas harder, an'—an' more important. This sort o' dyin' don't seem o' much account."

" No ? "

" That's it. I reckon, though, 'twould be other if I had a family round the bed. But there ain't none o' the boys left to stand by me now. It's hard."

" What's hard ? "

" Why, that two out o' the three should be called afore me. And hard is the manner of it. It's hard that, after Samuel died o' fever, Jim shud be blown up at Herodsfoot powder-mill. He made a lovely corpse, did Samuel; but Jim, you see, he hadn't a chance. An' as for William, he's never come home nor wrote a line since he joined the Thirty-Second ; an' it's little he cares for his home or his father. I reckoned, back along, 'Lizabeth, as you an' he might come to an understandin'."

" William's naught to me."

" Look here ! " cried the old man sharply ; " he treated you bad, did William."

" Who says so ? "

R

"Why, all the folks. Lord bless the girl! do 'ee think folks use their eyes without usin' their tongues? An' I wish it had come about, for you'd ha' kept en straight. But he treated you bad, and he treated me bad, tho' he won't find no profit o' that. You'm my sister's child, 'Lizabeth," he rambled on; "an' what house-room you've had you've fairly earned—not but what you was welcome: an' if I thought as there was harm done, I'd curse him 'pon my deathbed, I would."

"You be quiet!"

She turned from the window and cowed him with angry grey eyes. Her figure was tall and meagre; her face that of a woman well over thirty—once comely, but worn over-much, and prematurely hardened. The voice had hardened with it, perhaps. The old man, who had risen on his elbow in an access of passion, was taken with a fit of coughing, and sank back upon the pillows.

"There's no call to be niffy," he apologised at last. "I was on'y thinkin' of how you'd manage when I'm dead an' gone."

" I reckon I'll shift."

She drew a chair towards the bed and sat beside him. He seemed drowsy, and after a while stretched out an arm over the coverlet and fell asleep. 'Lizabeth took his hand, and sat there listlessly regarding the still shadows on the wall. The sick man never moved; only muttered once—some words that 'Lizabeth did not catch. At the end of an hour, alarmed perhaps by some sound within the bed's shadow, or the feel of the hand in hers, she suddenly pushed the curtain back, and, catching up the candle, stooped over the sick man.

His lids were closed, as if he slept still; but he was quite dead.

'Lizabeth stood for a while bending over him, smoothed the bedclothes straight, and quietly left the room. It was a law of the house to doff boots and shoes at the foot of the stairs, and her stocking'd feet scarcely raised a creak from the solid timbers. The staircase led straight down into the kitchen. Here a fire was blazing cheerfully, and as she descended

R 2

she felt its comfort after the dismal room above.

Nevertheless, the sense of being alone in the house with a dead man, and more than a mile from any living soul, was disquieting. In truth, there was room for uneasiness. 'Lizabeth knew that some part of the old man's hoard lay up-stairs in the room with him. Of late she had, under his eye, taken from a silver tankard in the tall chest by the bed such moneys as from week to week were wanted to pay the farm hands; and she had seen papers there, too—title-deeds, maybe. The house itself lay in a cup of the hill-side, backed with steep woods—so steep that, in places, anyone who had reasons (good or bad) for doing so, might well see in at any window he chose. And to Hooper's Farm, down the valley, was a far cry for help. Meditating on this, 'Lizabeth stepped to the kitchen window and closed the shutter; then, reaching down an old horse-pistol from the rack above the mantelshelf, she fetched out powder and bullet and fell to loading quietly, as one who knew the trick of it.

And yet the sense of danger was not so near

as that of loneliness—of a pervading silence
without precedent in her experience, as if its
master's soul in flitting had, whatever Scripture
may say, taken something out of the house with
it. 'Lizabeth had known this kitchen for a score
of years now; nevertheless, to-night it was
unfamiliar, with emptier corners and wider
intervals of bare floor. She laid down the
loaded pistol, raked the logs together, and set
the kettle on the flame. She would take comfort in a dish of tea.

There was company in the singing of the
kettle, the hiss of its overflow on the embers, and
the rattle with which she set out cup, saucer,
and teapot. She was bending over the hearth
to lift the kettle, when a sound at the door
caused her to start up and listen.

The latch had been rattled: not by the
wind, for the December night without was
misty and still. There was somebody on the
other side of the door; and, as she turned, she
saw the latch lowered back into its place.

With her eyes fastened on this latch, she set
down the kettle softly and reached out for her

pistol. For a moment or two there was silence. Then someone tapped gently.

The tapping went on for half a minute; then followed silence again. 'Lizabeth stole across the kitchen, pistol in hand, laid her ear against the board, and listened.

Yes, assuredly there was someone outside She could catch the sound of breathing, and the shuffling of a heavy boot on the door-slate. And now a pair of knuckles repeated the tapping, more imperiously.

" Who's there? "

A man's voice, thick and husky, made some indistinct reply.

'Lizabeth fixed the cap more securely on her pistol, and called again—

" Who's there? "

" What the devil——" began the voice.

'Lizabeth shot back the bolt and lifted the latch.

" If you'd said at once 'twas William come back, you'd ha' been let in sooner," she said quietly.

A thin puff of rain floated against her face

as the door opened, and a tall soldier stepped out of the darkness into the glow of the warm kitchen.

" Well, this here's a queer home-coming. Why, hullo, 'Lizabeth—with a pistol in your hand, too! Do you shoot the fatted calf in these parts now? What's the meaning of it?"

The overcoat of cinder grey that covered his scarlet tunic was powdered with beads of moisture; his black moustaches were beaded also; his face was damp, and smeared with the dye that trickled from his sodden cap. As he stood there and shook himself, the rain ran down and formed small pools upon the slates around his muddy boots.

He was a handsome fellow, in a florid, animal fashion; well-set, with black curls, dark eyes that yet contrived to be exceedingly shallow, and as sanguine a pair of cheeks as one could wish to see. It seemed to 'Lizabeth that the red of his complexion had deepened since she saw him last, while the white had taken a tinge of yellow, reminding her of the prize beef at the Christmas market last week. Somehow she could find nothing to say.

"The old man's in bed, I reckon. I saw the light in his window."

"You've had a wet tramp of it," was all she found to reply, though aware that the speech was inconsequent and trivial.

"Damnably. Left the coach at Fiddler's Cross, and trudged down across the fields. We were soaked enough on the coach, though, and couldn't get much worse."

"We?"

"Why, you don't suppose I was the only passenger by the coach, eh?" he put in quickly.

"No, I forgot."

There was an awkward silence, and William's eyes travelled round the kitchen till they lit on the kettle standing by the hearthstone.

"Got any rum in the cupboard?"

While she was getting it out, he took off his cap and great-coat, hung them up behind the door, and, pulling the small table close to the fire, sat beside it, toasting his knees. 'Lizabeth set bottle and glass before him, and stood watching as he mixed the stuff.

"So you're only a private."

William set down the kettle with some violence.

"You still keep a cursedly rough tongue, I notice."

"An' you've been a soldier five year. I reckoned you'd be a sergeant at least," she pursued simply, with her eyes on his undecorated sleeve.

William took a gulp.

"How do you know I've not been a sergeant?"

"Then you've been degraded. I'm main sorry for that."

"Look here, you hush up! Damn it! there's girls enough have fancied this coat, though it ain't but a private's; and that's enough for you, I take it."

"It's handsome."

"There, that'll do. I do believe you're spiteful because I didn't offer to kiss you when I came in. Here, Cousin 'Lizabeth," he exclaimed, starting up, "I'll be sworn for all your tongue you're the prettiest maid I've seen this five year. Give me a kiss."

" Don't, William ! "

Such passionate entreaty vibrated in her voice that William, who was advancing, stopped for a second to stare. Then, with a laugh, he had caught and kissed her loudly.

Her cheeks were flaming when she broke free.

William turned, emptied his glass at a gulp, and began to mix a second.

" There, there; you never look so well as when you're angered, 'Lizabeth."

" 'Twas a coward's trick," she panted.

" Christmas-time, you spitfire. So you ain't married yet ? Lord ! I don't wonder they fight shy of you; you'd be a handful, my vixen, for any man to tame. How's the old man ? "

" He'll never be better."

" Like enough at his age. Is he hard set against me ? "

" We've never spoke of you for years now, till to-night."

" To-night ? That's queer. I've a mind to tip up a stave to let him know I'm about. I will, too. Let me see—

" *When Johnny comes marching home again,*
Hooray ! hoo——"

"Don't, don't! Oh, why did you come back to-night, of all nights ? "

" And why the devil not to-night so well as any other ? You're a comfortable lot, I must say ! Maybe you'd like common metre better :—

" *Within my father's house*
The blessed sit at meat,
Whilst I my belly stay
With husks the swine did eat.

—" Why shouldn't I wake the old man ? I've done naught that I'm ashamed of."

" It don't seem you're improved by soldier-ing."

" Improved ? I've seen life." William drained his glass.

" An' got degraded."

" Burn your tongue ! I'm going to see him." He rose and made towards the door. 'Lizabeth stepped before him.

" Hush ! You mustn't."

" ' Mustn't ? ' That's a bold word."

"Well, then—'can't.' Sit down, I tell you."

"Hullo! Ain't you coming the mistress pretty free in this house? Stand aside. I've got something to tell him—something that won't wait. Stand aside, you she-cat!"

He pushed by her roughly, but she held on to his sleeve.

"It *must* wait. Listen to me."

"I won't."

"You shall. He's dead."

"*Dead!*" He reeled back to the table and poured out another glassful with a shaking hand. 'Lizabeth noticed that this time he added no water.

"He died to-night," she explained; "but he's been ailin' for a year past, an' took to his bed back in October."

William's face was still pallid; but he merely stammered—

"Things happen queerly. I'll go up and see him; I'm master here now. You can't say aught to that. By the Lord! but I can buy myself out—I'm sick of soldiering—and we'll settle down here and be comfortable."

" We ? "

His foot was on the stair by this time. He turned and nodded.

"Yes, *we*. It ain't a bad game being mistress o' this house. Eh, Cousin 'Lizabeth ?"

She turned her hot face to the flame, without reply; and he went on his way up the stairs.

'Lizabeth sat for a while staring into the wood embers with shaded eyes. Whatever the path by which her reflections travelled, it led in the end to the kettle. She remembered that the tea was still to make, and, on stooping to set the kettle back upon the logs, found it emptied by William's potations. Donning her stout shoes and pattens, and slipping a shawl over her head, she reached down the lantern from its peg, lit it, and went out to fill the kettle at the spring.

It was pitch-dark ; the rain was still falling, and as she crossed the yard the sodden straw squeaked beneath her tread. The yard had been fashioned generations since, by levelling back from the house to the natural rock of the hill-side, and connecting the two on the right by cow-house and stable, with an upper storey for barn and granary, on the left by a low wall, where, through a rough gate, the cart-track from the valley found its entrance. Against the further end of this wall leant an open cart-shed ; and within three paces of it a perpetual spring of water gushing down the rock was caught and arrested for a while in a stone trough before it hurried out by a side gutter, and so down to join the trout-stream in the valley below. The spring first came to light half-way down the rock's face. Overhead its point of emergence was curtained by a net-work of roots pushed out by the trees above and sprawling over the lip in helpless search for soil.

'Lizabeth's lantern threw a flare of yellow on these and on the bubbling water as she filled her kettle. She was turning to go when a sound arrested her.

It was the sound of a suppressed sob, and seemed to issue from the cart-shed. 'Lizabeth turned quickly and held up her lantern. Under the shed, and barely four paces from her, sat a woman.

The woman was perched against the shaft of a hay-waggon, with her feet resting on a mud-soiled carpet-bag. She made but a poor appealing figure, tricked out in odds and ends of incongruous finery, with a bonnet, once smart, hanging limply forward over a pair of light-coloured eyes and a very lachrymose face. The ambition of the stranger's toilet, which ran riot in cheap jewellery, formed so odd a contrast with her sorry posture that 'Lizabeth, for all her wonder, felt inclined to smile.

" What's your business here ? "

" Oh, tell me," whimpered the woman, "what's he doing all this time ? Won't his father see me ? He don't intend to leave me here all night, surely, in this bitter cold, with nothing to eat, and my gown ruined ! "

" He ? " 'Lizabeth's attitude stiffened with suspicion of the truth.

" William, I mean ; an' a sorry day it was I agreed to come."

" William ? "

"My husband. I'm Mrs. William Transom."

"Come along to the house." 'Lizabeth turned abruptly and led the way.

Mrs. William Transom gathered up her carpet-bag and bedraggled skirts and followed, sobbing still, but in *diminuendo*. Inside the kitchen 'Lizabeth faced round on her again.

"So you'm William's wife."

"I am; an' small comfort to say so, seein' this is how I'm served. Reely, now, I'm not fit to be seen."

"Bless the woman, who cares here what you look like? Take off those fal-lals, an' sit in your petticoat by the fire, here; you ain't wet through—on'y your feet; and here's a dry pair o' stockings, if you've none i' the bag. You must be possessed, to come trampin' over High Compton in them gingerbread things." She pointed scornfully at the stranger's boots.

Mrs. William Transom, finding her notions of gentility thus ridiculed, acquiesced.

"An' now," resumed 'Lizabeth, when her visitor was seated by the fire pulling off her

damp stockings, "there's rum an' there's tea.
Which will you take to warm yoursel'?"

Mrs. William elected to take rum, and 'Lizabeth noted that she helped herself with freedom.
She made no comment, however, but set about
making tea for herself; and, then, drawing up
her chair to the table, leant her chin on her
hand and intently regarded her visitor.

"Where's William?" inquired Mrs. Transom.

"Up-stairs."

"Askin' his father's pardon?"

"Well," 'Lizabeth grimly admitted, "that's
like enough; but you needn't fret about them."

Mrs. William showed no disposition to fret.
On the contrary, under the influence of the rum
she became weakly jovial and a trifle garrulous
—confiding to 'Lizabeth that, though married to
William for four years, she had hitherto been
blessed with no children; that they lived in
barracks, which she disliked, but put up with
because she doted on a red coat; that William
had always been meaning to tell his father, but
feared to anger him, "because, my dear," she
frankly explained, "I was once connected with

s

the stage "—a form of speech behind which 'Lizabeth did not pry; that, a fortnight before Christmas, William had made up his mind at last, " 'for,' as he said to me, 'the old man must be nearin' his end, and then the farm 'll be mine by rights; ' " that he had obtained his furlough two days back, and come by coach all the way to this doleful spot—for doleful she must call it, though she *would* have to live there some day—with no shops nor theayters, of which last it appeared Mrs. Transom was inordinately fond. Her chatter was interrupted at length with some abruptness.

"I suppose," said 'Lizabeth meditatively, " you was pretty, once."

Mrs. Transom, with her hand on the bottle, stared, and then tittered.

"Lud! my dear, you ain't over-complimentary. Yes, pretty I was, though I say it."

" We ain't neither of us pretty now—you especially."

" I'd a knack o' dressin'," pursued the egregious Mrs. Transom, " an' nice eyes an' hair. 'Why, Maria, darlin',' said William one day,

when him an' me was keepin' company, ' I
believe you could sit on that hair o' yours, I
do reely.' ' Go along, you silly ! ' I said, ' to be
sure I can.' "

" He called you darling ? "

" Why, in course.   H'ain't you never had a
young man ? "

'Lizabeth brushed aside the question by
another.

" Do you love him ?   I mean so that—that
you could lie down and let him tramp the life
out o' you ? "

" Good Lord, girl, what questions you do
ask !   Why, so-so, o' course, like other married
women.   He's wild at times, but I shut my
eyes ; an' he hav'n struck me this year past.   I
wonder what he can be doin' all this time."

" Come and see."

'Lizabeth rose.   Her contempt of this foolish, faded creature recoiled upon herself, until
she could bear to sit still no longer.   With
William's wife at her heels, she mounted the
stair, their shoeless feet making no sound.   The
door of the old man's bed-room stood ajar, and

s 2

a faint ray of light stole out upon the landing. 'Lizabeth looked into the room, and then, with a quick impulse, darted in front of her companion.

It was too late. Mrs. Transom was already at her shoulder, and the eyes of the two women rested on the sorry spectacle before them.

Candle in hand, the prodigal was kneeling by the dead man's bed. He was not praying, however; but had his head well buried in the oaken chest, among the papers of which he was cautiously prying.

The faint squeal that broke from his wife's lips sufficed to startle him. He dropped the lid with a crash, turned sharply round, and scrambled to his feet. His look embraced the two women in one brief flicker, and then rested on the blazing eyes of 'Lizabeth.

" You mean hound ! " said she, very slowly.

He winced uneasily, and began to bluster :

" Curse you ! What do you mean by sneaking upon a man like this ? "

" A man ! " echoed 'Lizabeth. " Man, then, if you will—couldn't you wait till your father was cold, but must needs be groping under his pillow for the key of that chest? You woman, there—you wife of this man— I'm main grieved you should have ha' seen this. Lord knows I had the will to hide it!"

The wife, who had sunk into the nearest chair, and lay there huddled like a half-empty bag, answered with a whimper.

"Stop that whining!" roared William, turning upon her, "or I'll break every bone in your skin."

"Fie on you, man! Why, she tells me you haven't struck her for a whole year," put in 'Lizabeth, immeasurably scornful.

"So, cousin, you've found out what I meant by 'we.' Lord! you fancied *you* was the one as was goin' to settle down wi' me an' be comfortable, eh? You're jilted, my girl, an' this is how you vent your jealousy. You played your hand well; you've turned us out. It's a pity —eh?—you didn't score this last trick."

"What do you mean?" The innuendo at the end diverted her wrath at the man's hateful coarseness.

" Mean ? Oh, o' course, you're innocent as a lamb ! Mean? Why, look here."

He opened the chest again, and, drawing out a scrap of folded foolscap, began to read :—

"*I, Ebenezer Transom, of Compton Bur-rows, in the parish of Compton, yeoman, being of sound wit and health, and willing, though a sinner, to give my account to God, do hereby make my last will and testament.*

"*My house, lands, and farm of Compton Burrows, together with every stick that I own, I hereby (for her good care of me) give and bequeath to Elizabeth Rundle, my dead sister's child*—Let be, I tell you ! "

But 'Lizabeth had snatched the paper from him. For a moment the devil in his eye seemed to meditate violence. But he thought better of it; and when she asked for the candle held it beside her as she read on slowly.

"*. . . . to Elizabeth Rundle, my dead sister's child, desiring that she may marry and bequeath the same to the heirs of her body; less* *the sum of one shilling sterling, which I command to be sent to my only surviving son William—"*

" You needn't go on," growled William.

" . . . . *because he's a bad lot, and he may so well know I think so. And to this I set my hand, this* 17*th day of September,* 1856.

> " *Signed*
>> "*EBENEZER TRANSOM.*
>
> " *Witnessed by*
>> " *JOHN HOOPER.*
>> " *PETER TREGASKIS.*"

The document was in the old man's handwriting, and clearly of his composition. But it was plain enough, and the signatures genuine. 'Lizabeth's hand dropped.

" I never knew a word o' this, William," she said humbly.

Mrs. Transom broke into an incredulous titter.

" Ugh ! get along, you designer ! "

" William," appealed 'Lizabeth, " I've never had no thought o' robbin' you."

'Lizabeth had definite notions of right and wrong, and this disinheritance of William struck her conservative mind as a violation of Nature's laws.

William's silence was his wife's opportunity.

"Robbery's the word, you baggage! You thought to buy him wi' your ill-got gains. Ugh! go along wi' you!"

'Lizabeth threw a desperate look towards the cause of this trouble—the pale mask lying on the pillows. Finding no help, she turned to William again—

"You believe I meant to rob you?"

Meeting her eyes, William bent his own on the floor, and lied.

"I reckon you meant to buy me, Cousin 'Lizabeth."

His wife tittered spitefully.

"Woman!" cried the girl, lapping up her timid merriment in a flame of wrath. "Woman, listen to me. Time was I loved that man o' your'n; time was he swore I was all to him. He was a liar from his birth. It's your natur' to think I'm jealous; a better woman would

know I'm *sick*—sick wi' shame an' scorn o'
mysel'. That man, there, has kissed me, oft'n
an' oft'n—kissed me 'pon the mouth. Bein'
what you are, you can't understand how those
kisses taste now, when I look at *you*."

" Well, I'm sure ! "

" Hold your blasted tongue ! " roared William. Mrs. Transom collapsed.

" Give me the candle," 'Lizabeth commanded. " Look here——"

She held the corner of the will to the flame,
and watched it run up at the edge and wrap the
whole in fire. The paper dropped from her hand
to the bare boards, and with a dying flicker was
consumed. The charred flakes drifted idly across
the floor, stopped, and drifted again. In dead
silence she looked up.

Mrs. Transom's watery eyes were open to
their fullest. 'Lizabeth turned to William and
found him regarding her with a curious frown.

" Do you know what you've done ? " he
asked hoarsely.

'Lizabeth laughed a trifle wildly.

" I reckon I've made reparation."

" There was no call——" began William.

" You fool—'twas to *myself!* An' now," she added quietly, " I'll pick up my things and tramp down to Hooper's Farm; they'll give me a place, I know, an' be glad o' the chance. They'll be sittin' up to-night, bein' Christmas time. Good-night, William! "

She moved to go; but, recollecting herself, turned at the door, and, stepping up to the bed, bent and kissed the dead man's forehead. Then she was gone.

It was the woman who broke the silence that followed with a base speech.

" Well! To think she'd lose her head like that when she found you wasn't to be had! "

" Shut up! " said William savagely; " an' listen to this: If you was to die to-night I'd marry 'Lizabeth next week."

*　　*　　*　　*　　*

Time passed. The old man was buried, and Mr. and Mrs. Transom took possession at Compton Burrows and reigned in his stead. 'Lizabeth dwelt a mile or so down the valley with the Hoopers, who, as she had said, were

thankful enough to get her services, for Mrs.
Hooper was well up in years, and gladly re-
signed the dairy work to a girl who, as she told
her husband, was of good haveage, and worth
her keep a dozen times over. So 'Lizabeth had
settled down in her new home, and closed her
heart and shut its clasps tight.

She never met William to speak to. Now
and then she caught sight of him as he rode past
on horseback, on his way to market or to the
"Compton Arms," where he spent more time and
money than was good for him. He had bought
himself out of the army, of course; but he retained his barrack tales and his air of having seen
life. These, backed up with a baritone voice and
a largehandedness in standing treat, made him
popular in the bar parlour. Meanwhile, Mrs.
Transom, up at Compton Burrows—perhaps
because she missed her "theayters"—sickened
and began to pine; and one January afternoon,
little more than a year after the home-coming,
'Lizabeth, standing in the dairy by her cream-
pans, heard that she was dead.

"Poor soul," she said; "but she looked a

sickly one." That was all. She herself wondered that the news should affect her so little.

"I reckon," said Mrs. Hooper with meaning,
"William will soon be lookin' round for another
wife."

'Lizabeth went quietly on with her skim-
ming.

It was just five months after this, on a warm
June morning, that William rode down the
valley, and, dismounting by Farmer Hooper's,
hitched his bridle over the garden gate, and
entered. 'Lizabeth was in the garden; he could
see her print sun-bonnet moving between the
rows of peas. She turned as he approached,
dropped a pod into her basket, and held out
her hand.

"Good day, William." Her voice was quite
friendly.

William had something to say, and 'Lizabeth quickly guessed what it was.

"I thought I'd drop in an' see how you was
gettin' on; for it's main lonely up at Compton
Burrows since the missus was took."

"I daresay."

"An' I'd a matter on my mind to tell you," he pursued, encouraged to find she harboured no malice. "It's troubled me, since, that way you burnt the will, an' us turnin' you out; for in a way the place belonged to you. The old man meant it, anyhow."

"Well," said 'Lizabeth, setting down her basket, and looking him full in the eyes.

"Well, I reckon we might set matters square, you an' me, 'Lizabeth, by marryin' an' settlin' down comfortable. I've no children to pester you, an' you're young yet to be givin' up thoughts o' marriage. What do 'ee say, cousin?"

'Lizabeth picked a full pod from the bush beside her, and began shelling the peas, one by one, into her hand. Her face was cool and contemplative.

"'Tis eight years ago, William, since last you asked me. Ain't that so?" she asked absently.

"Come, Cousin, let bygones be, and tell me; shall it be, my dear?"

"No, William," she answered; "'tis too late

an hour to ask me now. I thank you, but it can't be." She passed the peas slowly to and fro in her fingers.

"But why, 'Lizabeth?" he urged; "you was fond o' me once. Come, girl, don't stand in your own light through a bit o' pique."

"It's not that," she explained; "it's that I've found myself out—an' you. You've humbled my pride too sorely."

"You're thinking o' Maria."

"Partly, maybe; but it don't become us to talk o' one that's dead. You've got my answer, William, and don't ask me again. I loved you once, but now I'm only weary when I think o't. You wouldn't understand me if I tried to tell you."

She held out her hand. William took it.

"You're a great fool, 'Lizabeth."

"Good-bye, William."

She took up her basket and walked slowly back to the house; William watched her for a moment or two, swore, and returned to his horse. He did not ride homewards, but down the valley, where he spent the day at the " Compton Arms."

When he returned home, which was not before midnight, he was boisterously drunk.

Now it so happened that when William dismounted at the gate Mrs. Hooper had spied him from her bedroom window, and, guessing his errand, had stolen down on the other side of the garden wall parallel with which the peas were planted. Thus sheltered, she contrived to hear every word of the foregoing conversation, and repeated it to her good man that very night.

"An' I reckon William said true," she wound up. "If 'Lizabeth don't know which side her bread's buttered she's no better nor a fool—an' William's another."

"I dunno," said the farmer; "it's a queer business, an' I don't fairly see my way about in it. I'm main puzzled what can ha' become o' that will I witnessed for th' old man."

"She's a fool, I say."

"Well, well; if she didn't want the man I reckon she knows best. He put it fairly to her."

"That's just it, you ninny!" interrupted his wiser wife; "I gave William credit for more sense. Put it fairly, indeed! If he'd said nothin', but just caught her in his arms, an' clipped an' kissed her, she couldn't ha' stood out. But he's lost his chance, an' now she'll never marry."

And it was as she said.

THE END.